The Horse
in the Kitchen

The Horse
in the Kitchen

Stories of a Mexican-American Family

Ralph M. Flores

University of New Mexico Press
Albuquerque

© 2004 by the University of New Mexico Press
All rights reserved.
First Edition

Library of Congress Cataloging-in-Publication Data

Flores, Ralph M.
The horse in the kitchen : stories of a Mexican-American
family / Ralph M. Flores.— 1st ed.
  p. cm.
  ISBN 0-8263-3366-4 (cloth : alk. paper)
 1. Sonora (Mexico : State)—Social life and customs—Fiction.
 2. Arizona—Social life and customs—Fiction.
 3. Mexican American families—Fiction.
 4. Agricultural laborers—Fiction.
 5. Mexican Americans—Fiction.
 6. Poor families—Fiction.
 7. Depressions—Fiction.
 8. Immigrants—Fiction.
 I. Title.
PS3606.L6H67 2004
813´.6—dc22

                                    2003022127

Printed and bound in the U.S.A. by Thomson-Shore, Inc.
Body type set in Adobe Caslon 11/13.5
Display type set in Caslon Antique
Design and composition by Maya Allen-Gallegos

Para mi padre: Rafael Corrales Flores
Mentor, Role Model, Quiet Hero

Acknowledgments

Thanks to Beth Hadas and to Patrick Houlihan for reading the manuscript and giving encouragement, and special thanks to my wife, Geri M. Rhodes, whose help and advice have been invaluable.

Contents 🐎

Preface

I grew up with stories my father told of his childhood in Mexico and of his coming to America. They were tales of joy and sorrow, of laughter and pain, but no matter whether the subject was happy or sad, they always had the air of adventure stories wherein the events were the bits that made up the mosaic of a life, a life as a work-in-progress. His stories were never angry or bitter, but rather had a feeling of wonder at all the things that come together to make up the whole of a man's life. The stories became engrained in my childhood imagination, and the village, the people, seemed almost as real to me as those whom I saw daily.

His stories were the inspiration for the tales that follow. I have used his stories to create my own Mexican village peopled with individuals from my imagination, and to create a particular family and their odyssey to a new homeland. Although my stories have their roots in Dad's life, this is a work of fiction, and the narrator is not my father. I have, however, tried to imbue the narrator with some of my father's virtues: strength, wisdom, endurance, shrewdness, love, and a basic integrity and goodness as a human being. These same virtues have made me try to emulate my father, made me try to be the kind of man that he has been and continues to be.

Ultimately, these stories are a token of my love. Though I can never fully express in words what I feel for him, these tales are a gesture of my appreciation for all that he has been to me.

Prologue

My mother was seventeen when she married in 1900. She was born and brought up on a ranch in northern Sonora, Mexico, a few miles outside the village of La Virgen. At seventeen, Angelina Corrales Serrano was a beautiful *señorita* walking in the evening with some girl-friends around the village plaza, flirting secretly with the young men who were trying to impress the girls while pretending boredom and disinterest. The girls' parents sat or stood under the trees in the plaza, talking with neighbors, watching from the corners of their eyes, making sure the subdued courtship rituals of the young met with all the demands of propriety. One of those watching her promenade around the plaza was a visitor to La Virgen, a prospector who had come down from the mountains to have some rocks assayed and to replenish his supplies. He watched the seventeen-year-old closely, until her friends noticed and began giggling every time they passed near him. He was seen asking questions of some of the locals, and then he left.

His name was Ygnacio, and he began the courtship the following week, wooing her in keeping with the demands of custom. Arriving on horseback at the ranch, he visited with her parents while she peeked in from the next room. He was dark and formal, sitting on the edge of his seat, hands clasping his knees while he sweated nervously in the dark coat and tie he was obviously not used to wearing, earnestly explaining his desire to meet their daughter.

Her parents were shocked. He was, after all, ten years older than she was, and they still thought of her as little more than a child. They stammered and hawed, and eventually let him know they thought it "unusual" that a man of his age would desire to court their daughter. He answered that he was an honorable man with honorable intentions. They said they would consider his request and escorted him out the door.

Then began the arguments and the shouting. She was intrigued by him and was flattered that an "older man" should be interested in her as a woman. But her parents were unbending. He was an unknown, a stranger, a mature man, and she was little more than a naive child. No, he would not be allowed to visit her.

He kept trying. He would ride out to the ranch, and they would feel obligated by the demands of courtesy to invite him in. She was not supposed to be present, but she would always manage to appear, even if only for a few minutes to offer a glass of cool water or to ask some innocuous question. After he left, the shouts and accusations would begin. "You're encouraging him," they would shout, "even when you know the situation is impossible!"

"Ygnacio's a good man," she would respond, "and there's nobody in La Virgen I'm interested in."

Once, in desperation, her parents took her away to another village and left orders at the ranch that no one was to tell the suitor where they had gone. I guess they planned to stay away for a few months in the belief that he would lose hope and give up courting their daughter. Instead, he hung around the ranch wheedling the ranch hands and generally making a nuisance of himself until someone finally revealed where she had been taken. The next day, much to her parents' astonishment, he appeared at their front door, grimy and disheveled from having ridden all night, requesting permission to visit their daughter. So once again there were the uncomfortable visits in the parlor and the arguments afterward.

I was never able to determine exactly how it happened, but somehow the suitor and his beloved got together and made an escape plan. He rode in one night, she climbed out the window, and they rode off together and got married in a civil ceremony in Santa Maria. My future father quit prospecting and used his grubstake to buy a combination bar and pool hall and a grocery store, and they set up house in San Cristobal in northern Sonora. Within a year he was elected *comisario*, a position analogous to mayor in an American town. Her parents ultimately relented and accepted him as a son-in-law, as long as they had a church wedding. Eventually they realized he really was a good man, and they even grew to like him.

They had ten children, of which I was the fifth, born in 1908, two years before the Mexican Revolution began, that tumultuous upheaval of the Mexican *campesino* against the moneyed class and foreigners. The Revolution almost destroyed the civil infrastructure, creating anarchy and chaos in the countryside. Things got so bad that we fled our homeland, along with thousands of other Mexicans, and emigrated to the United States in search of a new home and a new life.

These are some memories of my childhood in Mexico, my immigration to this country, and my becoming an American.

⚘ El Pueblo

I was a four-year-old boy when we moved to San Cristobal, a small town in northern Sonora, Mexico. Now, many years later and many miles away, in my mind I am once again a child, standing on one of the foothills to the east of town from where I can see the entire community and outlying homes and ranches laid out before me like some wondrous scale-model toy. From this vantage point I can see my own home at the southeastern edge of town with two large cottonwoods, a chicken coop, storage shed, and pens in the back. My mother and my sister Teresa are hanging clothes on the line behind the house while my brother Antonio feeds the chickens and another brother, Roberto, slops a hog being fattened for slaughter in the coming winter. Maria Elena, another sister, is in the vegetable garden in the front yard. They are small, toy-like; they are shouting and laughing, but at this height and at this distance in time I cannot hear them except in fading memory.

Main Street in San Cristobal runs toward me, an unpaved track that curves toward the south after leaving town, disappearing in the far horizon, heading toward Santa Ana, some thirty-five miles away. The street, lined with hitching posts and storefronts, is wide enough to allow two horse-drawn wagons to pass comfortably. From this hilltop I cannot see the ruts left in the street by the wagon wheels, but I know that they are there. I know that when it rains the street becomes a gooey, muddy mess through which horses wheeze and strain as they pull a laden wagon.

I can see from here the miniature people walking in the middle of the street to chat or argue, or waving greetings at one another. Someone is entering my dad's little grocery store at the western end of town, or maybe entering the store of his main competitor, El Chino Li, the Chinaman who owns the combination grocery and mercantile store at the east end of town. Father's pool hall/cantina is next door to his grocery store, and across the street is his office, the office of the *comisario*—the mayor—the place from where Father was to set out on the first automobile ride taken by a town resident. I can see the Chinaman's house a block north of his store, where he lived with Emilia, his deaf-mute wife, and the huge cottonwood in his backyard under which we ate the "spirit food," and not far from there, the street where he was murdered.

At the far side of town a train is pulling into the station, so it must be Tuesday, Friday, or Sunday, the only days the train comes to San Cristobal. This is the end of the line, so the engine will be switched, and the train will pull out, heading west across the northern Sonora Desert to distant Hermosillo. San Cristobal is lucky to have a train station, a leftover from the days when the town was at its peak, when copper, silver, and some gold were being mined in the *sierras* east of town, and the trains would haul out the ore. The mines have pretty much played out, but a few die-hard operations remain, struggling for subsistence, and there is a fairly steady trickle of individual prospectors passing through town and buying supplies on their way to the rugged mountains to try their luck.

A few kids are playing on the tree-lined plaza in the middle of town, one block north of Main Street. The plaza is the heart of the community, where every evening the people gather after supper and sit on the wrought-iron benches to chat while the small kids run around shouting and the older kids flirt. It is the exchange center for all news and gossip. There are houses and stores all around the plaza, and over there, behind one of these homes, I can see Jesus Martinez's house with the pit Elutherio's bull fell into.

From here the predominant colors are the white of the squat, whitewashed adobe buildings, designed with few windows to keep out the summer heat and the winter cold, and the brown, foot-thick layer of dirt on the flat roofs for insulation and for soaking up the water when it rains. Sprinkled throughout is the green of the trees and shrubs in town. A few of the more prominent citizens have homes built entirely of wood, much more expensive than adobe, and much hotter in summer and colder in winter, but conferring on their owners a certain status. I can just make out the prime status home in the area, the ranch house of Fermino Réal, who runs more head of cattle than anyone else and is therefore accounted the town's wealthiest citizen: two stories, all wood.

To the south I can see the tree-lined Rio Verde, which arises in the sierras and snakes its way west to empty into the distant Pacific. The land around is checkered with the fields of green from the small farms irrigated by the ditches that tap into the river. Not far from the green *bosque* alongside the river, I can see the house of my

3

friends, Enrique and his brother Chencho. And not far from there, behind their parents' house, sits the shack of Fidelio Padilla, the greatest wood-carver in all of Mexico.

Ranching is the main industry here. There are still large sections of open rangeland where ranchers graze their cattle in common. Every spring the *vaqueros* round up the cattle and sort out the various brands so the owners can claim their herds and brand the new calves. And there are the usual businesses that any community has. Several cantinas, including my dad's, are strung along Main Street, but the rowdier bars, where the prostitutes ply their trade, are off the side streets at the edge of town. I can see the livery stable, the cobbler's shop, a *taqueria*, the butcher's, the bakery with its smells of fresh baked *bolillos*—delicious hot rolls—and pastries: *pan de huevo, biscochitos,* and the gingerbread *cochitos*. On one side of my dad's cantina is his small grocery store; on the other side, the tortilla factory, where every afternoon at four you can go see the girls rolling the corn *masa* into balls and pressing them into the round tortillas that sell for a few *centavos* a dozen.

Like small towns everywhere, San Cristobal seems sleepy, even half-dead, on the surface, but underneath are the usual human passions that keep excitement and gossip at a surprisingly high level. Adding to the excitement is the Mexican Revolution itself, which is swirling all around the little town and the entire nation of Mexico. After 1915, as Pancho Villa's Great Army of the North retreats and disintegrates, bands of Villa supporters and self-proclaimed revolutionaries occasionally ride through town, looting, looking for money, horses, guns, and taking anything they desire, often at gunpoint. Every now and then there is a "major event," and the entire town is in turmoil: the flood of 1915, when the Rio Verde overran its banks and Main Street became a channel of swiftly flowing water with squealing kids floating past Father's pool hall in wooden wash tubs, while worried adults prepared corn, beans, and tortillas to take with them, should the river rise more and they have to abandon the town to higher ground; the battle fought between revolutionary forces in 1917, some ten miles outside of town; and of course, the Great Race of 1916 between Fermino Réal's chestnut and the bay from Canitullo.

This place, these people come to me now across the years, sometimes as clearly as if I had seen them just yesterday. My childhood there was not idyllic, but it was a childhood of high intensity, sometimes good, sometimes frightening, but always memorable to me.

⟶ Quién Vive?

I awoke to the sound of voices. I opened my eyes and was looking up at a starry sky with no idea where I was. I heard an unfamiliar voice and turned toward it. In the moonlight I could see the silhouette of a man wearing a broad sombrero astride a horse. He held in one hand the dark form of a rifle, pointed downward at a man I now recognized as my father standing in front of the horse in his underwear. Now I remembered where I was. I was four years old and my family had moved to San Cristobal the day before. My father had bought a house at the edge of town, but it was too filthy and warm to sleep in, so we were all sleeping on the ground in the front yard. I had no idea who the man on horseback was or why he was threatening my father.

My father was talking. "I tell you, I don't know where you can buy beef for your men. We arrived here just yesterday and don't know anyone."

I heard a horse snort a few feet away, and when I looked I saw the dark shapes of a group of men on horses.

"Don't lie to me, man," said the one with the rifle. "We need food. We will pay for the beef." The rifle didn't waver.

"Look," said Father, "all our possessions are in the wagon. The house has no doors or windows. It's empty. We just arrived. We don't know anyone here."

The man sat immobile on his horse, as if frozen or stone. Now I could feel the tension all around me as I noticed the rest of the family sitting up stiff and motionless in the moonlight. Only Ernesto, the youngest, remained sleeping. The saddle creaked as the man leaned forward a little, still pointing the rifle at Father.

"*¿Quién vive?*" he asked, his voice soft and menacing.

Father looked up at him without responding. It was a dangerous question, a question literally of life or death. He was being asked to which side in the Revolution he gave his allegiance, Villa or Carranza. In the darkness there was no way to judge whom these men followed.

"Look at us," said Father. "We are humble people struggling to make a living. We know nothing of politics or any of these matters."

"*¿Quién vive?*" he repeated. This time his voice was not as soft.

"We know nothing of the Revolution." My mother's voice came out of the darkness. "These are very hard times, and we must devote all our time and strength to feeding and sheltering our children. We do not know who is fighting whom. We wish only for peace."

The one on horseback turned toward the voice, but his rifle did not move. He turned back to Father. "Is this your woman?"

"Yes. She is the mother of my children."

He sat still, as if pondering a particularly troublesome problem.

"*¿Qué hacemos, Jefe?*" asked one from the group standing to the side, wanting to know what they should do now.

7

Their chief moved quickly, slipping the rifle into its scabbard and yanking the reins. "*¡Vámonos muchachos!*" He turned and rode off toward town, followed by his troops.

We all sat unmoving, watching as they disappeared in the night. My mother leaned forward, resting her head on her arms crossed over her knees, as if totally exhausted. My dad turned and moved toward us kids.

"Is everything all right now?" I asked. Father bent down, picked me up and held me.

"Yes," he said, "everything is all right. Everybody cover up and go back to sleep." He laid me down and spread the blanket over me.

It took me a while to fall asleep. I finally drifted off, lulled by my parents' voices talking in low, intense whispers.

Elutherio's Bull

My brother Roberto and I were playing tag with several other kids on the plaza when a boy came running across the plaza screaming: "*¡El Diablo! ¡Hay viene el Diablo!*" The Devil was coming! In the middle of the street behind him, swiveling his massive head, stood a big black bull. "*¡El Diablo!*" the boy shouted again. The bull trotted onto the plaza, his tail swishing savagely. The plaza emptied immediately, shrieking children scattering in all directions. For just a second the bull stood, swinging its horns from side to side, then galloped after Roberto and me as we fled toward Main Street. I could hear the hoarse, rasping breath of El Diablo behind us as we sped around the corner toward Father's cantina.

Elutherio Ramirez had the meanest bull in San Cristobal. He kept it pastured in a field behind his house at the northern edge of town, and for twenty *pesos*, a rancher could have a cow covered by El Diablo in hopes of improving his herd. El Diablo was particularly mean with children since we kids would regularly test our courage by going into his pasture and teasing him, and when he charged us, we would roll under the bottom strand of the barbed-wire fence where we could

9

continue to tease him in safety. Now, the bull had a chance for a payback.

We ran to Father's cantina, tumbled through the swinging doors, and stood panting in the middle of the cool, dark interior. "*¡El Diablo! El Diablo!*" we shouted at the surprised and confused customers. One of the men hurried to the door and looked out in time to see the bull turn and start back up the street.

"*¡Aye jodido!* Elutherio's bull is loose! *¡El Diablo!*" Everyone in the cantina ran out into the street shouting excitedly. The bull turned quickly and came trotting toward us. Just as quickly we turned as one and ran back to the cantina, where people were jamming up in the doorway trying to get in at once. In a few seconds we were all back in, everyone talking loudly at the same time.

The bull turned off Main onto the alley between Father's cantina and the tortilla factory, heading back toward the plaza. One of the men in the cantina stuck his head out the door, and seeing the bull trot off, stepped outside, followed by everyone else in the bar. The crowd of men trailed the bull toward the plaza at a safe distance. Roberto and I followed behind, while a number of people ran out of the stores and bars on Main Street and joined us.

Quite a few people had already heard about the escaped bull and were congregating on the plaza when El Diablo trotted into view. There was a general shout as the bull lowered his head and charged at the knot of people closest to him. That little group burst into fragments flying in all directions, screaming. My friend Ramiro tripped in front of a burrito stand, and the bull, seeing him, swerved in his direction. Lazarillo Madero distracted the bull from Ramiro by running at it and leaping nimbly over a hitching post when the bull chased him. Emilia, the deaf-mute, wandered onto the plaza, curious about the crowd that gathered at midday. She couldn't hear the warnings shouted at her by the crowd, and by the time she saw El Diablo he had lowered his head and was getting ready to charge. Her husband, the Chinaman Li, came running out of the crowd waving his white apron at the bull and shouting shrilly in Chinese. When the bull ran at him, he turned and ran back toward the crowd, which immediately dissolved. I saw someone dragging Doña Luisa off the street by her arms. This much-respected and despised moral judge of the community was sputtering angrily at the indignity.

By now the bull was quite confused. There were so many targets he couldn't decide which ones to attack, so he stood in the plaza, first turning one way and then the other, pawing at the ground and snorting. Then he turned and came running at the group I was standing with. Someone grabbed me and carried me off, depositing me in the doorway of one of the stores encircling the plaza.

"Stay here," said my father, then he turned and ran in the direction the bull had gone. El Diablo had left the plaza, which was emptying of people as they followed behind. I saw my friend Enrique, three years older than I was, among the crowd, so I left my secure doorway and ran after him. Every now and then I would hear a roar from the crowd, which told me that the bull had turned and charged again. I caught up with Enrique as the narrow street opened up into empty lots and scattered houses.

"Look!" shouted Enrique. "He's over there!" He was gesturing toward the house of Jesus Martinez.

I could see El Diablo standing atop a mound of dirt from a pit Jesus had dug in his backyard. Originally, Jesus had started digging a well, but after he dug a hole about six feet deep, he changed his mind and decided to dig a root cellar instead. He dug a little deeper and enlarged the hole until it was about six feet square. Then he changed his mind again and decided he would turn it into a house, most of it below ground level to be warm in winter and cool in summer. So he enlarged it until it was about eight feet square and seven feet deep, and then he gave up on his project altogether. Now it was just "Jesus's pit," part of his backyard. It was on the dirt from this pit that the bull was standing, glaring balefully down at the people following him.

Enrique and I were elbowing our way through the crowd toward him when I heard him bellow. The bull was struggling to maintain his balance as he slowly slid down the dirt pile toward the pit. Then he disappeared behind the mound. There was shouting from the crowd and it surged forward toward the pit. El Diablo lay at the bottom on his side, struggling to get up. Evidently the fall had knocked the wind out of him. He staggered up and stood swaying, wobbly for a few minutes, staring up at the crowd of people ringing the pit.

By now Elutherio himself had arrived to find his bull standing some seven feet below the surface of the ground.

"Elutherio!" people shouted. "We got your bull! We captured him for you!"

Elutherio stood a moment, looking down at his bull. "You captured him, eh? And how are we going to get him out?"

There was silence as people considered this new problem. El Diablo must have weighed at least a thousand pounds.

"We need some rope," someone suggested, "to tie around him and pull him up."

"And will you be the one to go into the pit and tie it around him?" someone snickered.

"I'll do it!" shouted Chapo Miguel, already more than slightly drunk. He straightened his five-foot-two-inch frame as much as he could in his drunken state. "I'm not afraid of anything or anyone! Bring me some rope and I'll tie it around that *jodido*." He started scrambling up the mound of dirt.

Ramon Padilla—father of Fidelio the wood-carver— himself a bit tipsy and already atop the mound with his back to the pit, grabbed Chapo, trying to stop him and push him back down.

"*¡Oye loco!* Stay down there before you get yourself killed!"

Chapo kept coming, pushing at Ramon, who lost his balance and started slipping down the other side of the mound toward the pit. Someone grabbed him just as he was about to topple into it, and they both teetered on the brink for a moment. Regaining his balance, the hot-tempered Ramon was in a rage, screaming at Chapo, who was now standing on the mound.

"I'll get you *cabrón!* I'll teach you to fool with Ramon Padilla!" He started back up toward Chapo but someone grabbed him and held on while several others took hold of Chapo and hustled him back into the crowd.

"Get a rope," someone said. "We still need a rope to get the bull out."

"A rope won't do any good without some poles to make a frame to put across the pit and run the rope over to haul him up. I'll go get some poles."

"We don't need any poles or frame," someone else argued. "We need two ropes to run under the bull, and then everyone grab hold of the ends of the rope and pull him out."

"We need a sling," another shouted, "to place under his belly, and then we can pull him up."

"Just how the hell are we going to put a sling under his belly?"

By now everyone was trying to out-shout everyone else, but no one was doing anything. The crowd was breaking up into small groups arguing over what was the best thing to do, and a few individuals were getting red-faced and threatening. When the din subsided a bit while people caught their breaths, the voice of my friend Enrique could be heard clearly.

"I know an easy way to get the bull out," he said.

Everybody turned to him.

"Put dirt into the pit," he said, "and fill it up until the bull can get out."

Total silence. Then, "Let's go get some shovels!" People scattered, running to their houses and coming back with shovels, and in a few cases, buckets. They fell to work with a will, dumping dirt into one end of the pit, raising the level, and then filling up the other end, forcing the bull up to the higher level. This process continued until, after several minutes of struggle, the bull gave a mighty heave and was out of the pit. He promptly lowered his head and charged at those nearest him. There was a loud roar as the crowd parted, dropping shovels and buckets. The bull ran on, back toward the plaza, with the yelling crowd following at a distance.

In a moment Enrique and I were the only ones at the pit, standing on what was left of the mound of earth. After the tumult there was silence, broken every now and then by a distant shout from the crowd.

Enrique looked at me and grinned. "*Pues, se fueron todos al Diablo.*" They had all gone to the Devil.

We giggled and sat throwing clods of earth into the pit.

🌺 Election Day

Before we made our move to San Cristobal, Father had come and bought our home, a pool hall/cantina, and a small grocery store, using the money he had saved up from his days as a prospector before he married and from his job afterward as a foreman on a ranch outside La Virgen. About a year after our move, he became the *comisario,* an office with combined duties of mayor, magistrate, police force, and jailor. None of these responsibilities took much effort or time to fulfill. In a small, isolated community like San Cristobal the major function of the magistrate was to fine people for disturbing the peace, usually a result of public drunkenness. As the town policeman—more like a sergeant-at-arms, really—Father had the right to carry a revolver, but the official handgun was broken and wouldn't fire, so he kept it locked in the safe in his office. The only real armed threat was from the bands of revolutionaries that occasionally rode through town looking for guns, money, and horses. The jail was connected to the comisario's office by a heavy wood door. It was a small room with thick adobe walls and two small windows about seven feet above floor level, secure enough for its major function—to let drunks sleep off their intoxication without being a nuisance to others or a danger to themselves.

Father did not want to be comisario, but was sort of pushed into it, *drafted* one might say. Avenício Romero, the man Father replaced, had gotten so old and feeble—in addition to being nearly blind—that he was unable to fulfill the few responsibilities the position required of him, so he was talked into retirement.

There were no official "elections" for the post in San Cristobal, but when the position was vacant there was an open meeting of the men in town, held in one of the cantinas, where after some debate and downing of drinks, a new comisario would be installed by acclamation. Since the comisario usually held the position for quite a while—until he died, left town, grew too old to serve, or until people just got tired of him—there was no need for a more efficient system. After enough drinks and discussion, there was always consensus. The job brought no salary, but the magistrate did get to keep whatever fines he collected from lawbreakers. However, if the people felt he collected too many fines, there would be another gathering in a cantina to replace him.

After Avenício announced his retirement, the meeting to elect a new official was held in Father's cantina. By tradition, the saloon owner provided the first round of drinks on the house, so people made a point to arrive on time. After the first round of drinks, customers paid the usual price for a drink, and since the place was packed, it was a busy and profitable day for the *cantinero*. So Father and two employees were working behind the bar while the election was being held. Antonio, seven years older than me, was put to work collecting glasses and wiping tables. Roberto and I sat in a corner, out of the way, watching.

In the noisy confusion of the cantina, we could hear the names of Fermino Réal and Elutherio Ramirez mentioned most frequently. Elutherio was a good man, but he had a serious handicap in that he was illiterate, and there were many who felt it useful to have a comisario who could read and write. Don Fermino had the advantage of being well known and respected, and of owning a revolver that actually fired, but he came with the disadvantage of being too wealthy and influential. Many people did not trust him and were concerned that he might use the position to his advantage in some vague, unspecified way. So, like a deadlocked political convention, there was a lot of talking and shouting, but no decision-making. Those others interested in becoming candidates did not want to announce too soon and run the risk of not getting the acclamation needed to win.

Fermino Réal obviously wanted the job and was liberal with his money in buying drinks, but many still held back from him. Every now and then someone would stand and try to call for a decision, but he would be shouted down. Then more tequila would be drunk, accompanied by increasingly loud debate, and then another call for a decision, which would be shouted down.

At one point in the process, one of Elutherio's supporters was about to come to blows with one of Don Fermino's supporters. Father quickly came around the bar and stepped between the two antagonists, and in a few minutes had them shaking hands and sitting back down. As Father headed back behind the bar, Solario, the butcher with an immense moustache, grabbed him by the arm.

"*Oyé, compadre,* why don't you become our next *comisario?*" Solario stood on a chair before Father could protest. "Listen!" he shouted. The cantina quieted down. "What about Ygnacio here? He's an honest man, and he gets along with people. Why not him?"

There was a moment's silence, and then chaos as everyone started talking. It was becoming clear to everyone: a dark horse had entered the race and was on the inside rail headed for victory.

"I speak for Ygnacio!" someone shouted. Suddenly everyone seemed to be yelling, "Ygnacio, Ygnacio," and in a few seconds, Father had become the new comisario.

Now that he had been elected, Father felt obligated to have another round of drinks on the house for everyone, an act that immediately reinforced people's certainty that they had elected the right man.

By the time the cantina emptied and the electors had staggered out into the street, it was almost time for supper. Antonio, Roberto, Father, and I walked home down Main Street. Everything looked a little different to me now from a few hours before, now that my dad was the town's only elected official.

"Oh Lord," Father muttered. "As if I didn't have enough to do already. How am I going to explain this to your mother?"

When he told her he was the new comisario, her immediate response was, "As if you didn't have enough to do already!" But I could tell from the way she fussed over him at supper that she was proud of him and pleased that others could see in him the virtues she knew to be his.

El Chino

The Chinaman first came to San Cristobal in 1914, when I was about six years old. He was the first Chinese to come live in our little Mexican town and immediately became the source of curiosity and lots of talk. Everyone called him "El Chino Li." I don't know where he lived before he came to San Cristobal, but he did speak Spanish, although with a funny accent. He had enough money to buy a house and open up a business, a small grocery and mercantile store, which competed in some ways with Father's grocery store on the other side of town, but most of our income came from the pool hall and cantina Father also ran.

Much to everyone's surprise, about a year after he arrived, Li married Emilia Robles, a girl from one of the ranches outside town. Nobody suspected that Li ever even talked to any of the eligible girls, much less courted one. But Emilia was a muda, a deaf-mute, and this probably had something to do with the quick marriage. Her parents were sure she would never find a husband, so when Li asked for her hand they consented gladly, even if he was a Chinaman.

Emilia moved into town, and together they ran the store, with Li handling the customers. She was slender and shy, and I thought she was pretty, with her long black hair pulled into a *trenza*, the shiny braid that hung heavy on her shoulders and back. Li always talked to her in a normal voice, often in Chinese, as if he thought she could hear and understand him. She would smile at him whenever she saw he was talking to her, and I used to think that somehow she did hear and understand.

The two soon became accepted members of the community, and we townspeople saw nothing stranger in them than we saw in Reyes, the blind man who slept in the shed behind the Lopezes' house and lived on what people gave him, or in Martin, the son of Elisa and Juan Carrion, a mentally retarded man who walked the streets hooting at people. They were all part of us.

One evening my brother Roberto came running to report that El Chino was doing something strange in his backyard. We sneaked up and peeked between the boards of his fence. The yard was empty, but under the huge cottonwood in back we could see a number of bowls, plates, and cups arranged around the tree trunk. The plates and bowls were covered with squares of white cloth.

"I saw him coming out and leaving that stuff under the tree," whispered Roberto. "I hid here and watched him going into the house and coming out with more . . ."

Roberto stopped talking when we heard the back door shut. El Chino had stepped out and was walking back toward the tree carrying two plates, also covered with cloth. He was dressed the way the people dressed in some old pictures from China that I had seen. Instead of his usual cotton pants, shirt, and apron, he was wearing blue silk pants and shirt and a round silk cap. He knelt under the tree and set the two plates down with the others, and then he bowed until his forehead touched the ground. He stayed that way for a few moments, then straightened, got up, and walked back into the house.

Roberto and I waited until it got dark, but Li did not come out again.

We ran to the house of our friends, the brothers Chencho and Enrique. Chencho was my age, while Enrique was three years older, and one year older than Roberto. After we described what we had seen, the four of us agreed to get together at ten that night and find out just what El Chino was putting under the tree. By then, all the hardworking, respectable people of San Cristobal were in bed, so Roberto and I were able to climb out the window without anyone knowing. This business with El Chino Li was a mystery we had to get to the bottom of.

Roberto and I arrived at Chencho and Enrique's house a few minutes after ten. Waiting at the gate were two other boys, the Martinez brothers, Ramiro and Pedro.

"What are you doing here?" asked Roberto.

"We're going with you," answered Ramiro. "Enrique told us about what you saw, and we want to go with you."

The Martinez family was the poorest in town and often depended on the charity of the people to survive. The father's leg had been crushed in a mining accident years before. There was not much work he was capable of doing. The oldest son, who at eighteen had been the main support of the family, had run away with a group of revolutionaries a year earlier. I could tell Roberto was not pleased that the two brothers were there, not because they were poor (we all were), but because Enrique had told anyone else at all.

Roberto was giving his grudging acceptance when Enrique and Chencho snuck up on us and made us all jump.

"Come on, let's go," said Enrique.

We climbed over Li's fence, noiseless like burglars, then moved to the cottonwood. When we uncovered the bowls, we discovered rice and chicken, rice and shrimp, and pork mixed with things we couldn't identify. The plates held fruit, cookies, and little round honey cakes topped with nuts; the cups held tea.

After we had uncovered everything, we sat still for a moment wondering what this meant. "Do you think he's crazy?" whispered Chencho.

"No," said Enrique, the oldest and most knowledgeable of the group. "I think it has something to do with his religion."

"Religion!" snorted Ramiro. "I never heard about this in church."

"Sssh! Not so loud," warned Enrique. "Chinamen don't go to church."

"Well, how can he have a religion and not go to church?" asked Ramiro. "Every religious person I know goes to church."

"Chinamen aren't Christians," Enrique explained. "It's against the law for them to be Christians. They have a different religion."

"How can anyone be religious and not be Christian?" asked Ramiro. "Do they worship the Devil?" he added in a frightened tone.

"Maybe this is a trick," said Roberto. "Maybe he put some poison in the food here, so that whoever eats it will die!"

This idea left everyone quiet for a moment.

"Maybe he's working for the revolutionaries and wants to kill everyone so they can get all the food and horses," said Ramiro.

"No," responded Roberto. "Revolutionaries hate *Chinos*. My father said that Pancho Villa always kills *Chinos* when he captures any."

"I think he left the food here for spirits to eat," offered Enrique.

"Spirits! Do you mean *ghosts?*" I asked. My heart was beating fast.

"I think he wants to feed the spirits of dead people he knows, like his family." Enrique sounded very reassuring.

"Do you think the food is poisoned?" Ramiro asked.

"No," answered Enrique.

Ramiro picked up a bowl of rice and meat, and without saying a word, grabbed a handful and stuffed it in his mouth. We watched in silence while he chewed. I was wondering if he was going to fall over and start moaning, but instead he looked at us and exclaimed, "*¡Chingado!* That's good!" He took another handful.

All at once we were grabbing whatever was closest to us and shoveling it into our mouths. I was eating things I had never tasted before, things I couldn't even name, but Ramiro was right: it was all delicious.

We quickly emptied all the bowls and started in on the plates of goodies. I grabbed a plate with sweet round cakes at the same moment Pedro, Ramiro's little brother, did. We were pulling on the plate, each one claiming it as his own, when Enrique grabbed my wrist. "Let him have it," he ordered.

I started to resist, but Enrique's hold was painful and I let go of the plate. Pedro jerked the plate away and started gulping down the cakes, hunched over, making little smacking sounds. I felt embarrassed for him.

When we had eaten our fill, we let Pedro and Ramiro take what was left. They filled their pockets with fruit and pastries, every now and then licking their fingers and moaning softly.

We got up to leave, but Enrique told us to pick up the bowls and plates and stack them up neatly. While we were doing this, he emptied all the cups of tea on the ground. He looked at us and said, "The spirits not only like to eat, they like to drink tea too." We all started giggling as we walked away from the tree.

The next morning I went back to Chencho's house, and the two of us walked over to Chino Li's. We peered through the fence, but all the utensils under the cottonwood were gone. There was no sign that anything had happened there last night. We went to Li's store and found him outside sweeping the wooden sidewalk in front of his store. I could see Emilia inside through the glass window. She smiled and waved. I waved back.

"Good morning, boys," beamed Li. "How are you today?"

"Fine, sir," we both answered.

"Are you hungry this morning? Would you like something special to eat?" he asked in his funny Spanish. "Yes?"

Chencho and I nodded.

He went in and came out with two of the round honey cakes topped with nuts. "Here," he said. "I bet you have never eaten anything like this before."

He watched us, grinning widely as we bit into the cakes. His eyes were sparkling, and he seemed to be enjoying a private joke. Emilia came to the door, smiling.

"Look here woman," Li said to Emilia. "These boys are tasting something they've never had before. Isn't that right, boys? Something completely new?" He looked at us closely, still grinning. I thought they were both going to burst out laughing.

Chencho and I gobbled down the cakes, gave our thanks, and hurried off.

"He knows," said Chencho. "He knows it was us that ate the food he put under the tree."

"But he's not angry," I responded. "If he knew, he would be mad."

"He knows," said Chencho, "he knows."

Chino Li never mentioned the food under the cottonwood, and he remained friendly to us, so we never knew for sure if he was aware of what had happened. But we checked his backyard regularly just in case more bowls and plates should appear under the tree, but none ever did.

Three months later a band of Pancho Villa's followers raided San Cristobal.

Ramiro brought the warning of the coming raid. He came running down the main street hollering that a group of horsemen was riding toward town. He had seen their dust from the foothills and had immediately run to warn everyone. By now, we all knew that a band of horsemen usually meant bad news for the townspeople since they would "requisition" supplies from us, taking anything they considered to be of value. So we would try to hide our possessions before they arrived.

As soon as we heard Ramiro, Roberto and I ran home to hide Charro, my dad's favorite horse. We ran to the corral behind the house and led Charro into the kitchen, where we always hid him during a raid. The revolutionaries never thought to look in the house for a horse. Mother was in the kitchen when we brought Charro in.

"Quick!" she said. "Go look for your father!"

Roberto ran off in one direction and I went in another. I found Father hurrying out of the pool hall as the first group of men rode into town, shooting their rifles and pistols in the air and shouting, "¡*Viva Villa!*"

As soon as he heard the shouts for Villa, Father grabbed me by the shoulders and told me to hurry and warn Chino Li to hide. I ran off Main Street and down the back alleys to the other end of town. I had just rounded the corner of Li's store when I saw him being led out the front door by a Villista who was holding a gun to his head. Li looked right at me, but he looked so terrified and confused that I don't think he recognized me. Li was led into the street, and soon there were several horsemen around him. One of them reached out with his boot and pushed Li in the chest, knocking him to the ground. I turned and ran to look for my dad.

He was coming down the street toward us, his face pale, his mouth a thin line. "Papa! We've got to help El Chino! They've got him and they're hurting him!"

There was a loud noise from Li's store. Some of the men had gone in and were throwing Li's merchandise through the large glass window out into the street. One of the horsemen grabbed a bolt of cloth and galloped down the street, unrolling and dragging the cloth behind him. I could see Li kneeling in the street with a gun pressed against the back of his head.

Father turned to me. "Go find Emilia, quick!" he said in a low, hard voice.

I ran to Li's house and banged on the door, shouting for Emilia. Then I remembered she was deaf and would not be able to hear me, so I ran into the house. It was empty. I ran into the backyard, but it was empty too. I was in a panic and could not think what to do next. I started to cry, but the thought that I had to find Emilia held back my tears, and I ran to the neighbors. They had no idea where Emilia was.

I ran wildly up and down the side streets of town, but she was nowhere to be seen. I ran back to the main street to tell Father I had failed to find Emilia. The wreckage of Li's store was still dumped in the middle of the street, but the people were gone. I stood there sobbing in fear when I heard some shots and shouting down one of the side streets. I ran toward the noise, and when I turned the corner, I saw a crowd of people in the street and a group of revolutionaries riding away shouting and shooting their weapons. I got to the crowd and pushed my way in toward the middle until I could see my father kneeling down by what had once been a man but was now a bloody mess with a rope around its neck. Someone grabbed me from behind and started pulling me back out of the crowd. It was Olga, my oldest sister.

We stood at the edge of the group, Olga with strands of hair pulled loose from her trenza, crying almost noiselessly, snot running down from her nose. "Quick," she said, "let's go home."

Then there was a gasp from the crowd. Someone shouted, "Here comes Emilia!"

Running down the street toward us was Emilia, her skirt billowing behind her, her mouth open, eyes wild. The crowd opened up like the seas parting and she fell by the bloody obscenity in the middle of the street.

"Come on, come on," wept Olga, pulling on my arm. "Let's go home."

I twisted around to look back as she pulled me away and the image burned in my memory: Emilia on her knees, her head thrown back in a savage, piercing, utterly soundless scream.

🌵 Automobile

Chencho, Roberto, and I were playing in our backyard when Enrique came running up, excited and out of breath.

"Come see," he shouted. "Quick!" He turned and ran out of the yard toward town.

We ran after him, shouting for him to wait up. He turned onto the main street running toward the village office. We could see a large crowd of people gathered around the front of the office, but not until we pushed our way into the crowd did we see what the center of attraction was. Standing there was a machine, a dusty contraption that looked a little like a black bathtub on four skinny rubber tires. Some of the villagers were delicately touching the machine, leaving shiny little trails through the pale dust that covered it. People were chattering in low, excited tones.

"It's an automobile!" said Refugio, who ran the livery stable. "I saw one in Hermosillo when I was there last month. Some people say they will replace horses, but that's the stupidest thing I ever heard."

"Can it go as fast as a horse?" someone asked.

Refugio laughed. "No way. Any good horse will leave it standing still in a race. They're just toys for the rich."

"Here comes the owner." The phrase was repeated like a chant as two strangers and my father walked out of the cantina toward the crowd. The crowd parted as the three men came through and entered the village office. The people crowded around the door, looking in as Father brought out a map and the three of them peered at it with Father running his finger along its surface. I could see them, but I couldn't hear a word they were saying. They shook hands and came back out as the crowd moved aside. The three of them went back into the cantina with the crowd trailing. Father brought out a bottle of tequila and they shared a drink.

Within a few minutes, everyone in the cantina knew why the strangers were there. The two men were prospectors who wanted to look for gold in the surrounding hills. After they arrived in town, they heard that Father had once been a prospector, before his marriage, and that he was familiar with the area around town. So they asked him for advice on likely places to look, and he agreed to go with them into the foothills the following morning. He would be the first townsperson to ride in a car.

At first, Father assumed that it would merely be a matter of getting in the car with the two men and driving off, but as the afternoon and evening wore on, it became clear to him that his being the first villager to ride in a car was in reality an event. The importance of the event was compounded by Father's being the village comisario. People came to our house all afternoon and evening to shake his hand and congratulate him and to get the exact time the event would occur.

The next morning the villagers were gathering on Main Street early, and others from the outlying ranches were beginning to drift in. By ten o'clock there was a sizeable crowd milling in the street. Father, Roberto, and I left home to go to the cantina where the two strangers had rented a room upstairs for the night. When we turned onto Main Street and Father saw the size of the crowd, he turned around and went back home. At first I thought he had a change of heart and was going to stay home, but instead he went in the house and put on his best clothes, a black broadcloth suit with a string tie and a gray Stetson hat, and shiny black shoes. The three of us then walked down the street to the cantina. Several people even cheered, making my thin chest swell with pride.

The two strangers were waiting outside the cantina and again shook Father's hand when we arrived. "Let's go," said one of them, and a murmur ran through the crowd.

People lined up along both sides of the street and the driver got into the front seat of the car. Father got in behind him, sitting on the back rim of the car, his legs dangling down behind the front seat. The other man went in front of the car and began turning the crank. Suddenly the machine erupted in coughs and belches and sat there shaking and rattling as the crowd broke into applause. The other man got into the car and settled into his seat.

For a few seconds they all sat there in the noisy contraption while the crowd held its breath. Suddenly, as if someone had given it a pull on a rope, the car jerked forward. It started down the street, but the unexpected lurch had sent Father into a backward flip that deposited him face down in the middle of the street. The crowd let out a great "Ooh" and stood in stunned silence. Father lay perfectly still, spread-eagled, face down, his Stetson upside down beside him. The car went about ten feet and came to a stop.

Father stood up slowly, retrieved his hat, and slapped it against his pants and coat, releasing clouds of tan dust. The crowd remained silent as Father put the hat back on his head. He faced the crowd on one side of the street, removed the hat and did a deep bow. He then turned to the other side and repeated the act. "That's the way I always get out of automobiles," he announced loudly. The crowd broke into a roar of laughter and applause.

He got back into the car, but this time he held on tightly to the side of the auto with both hands. The car went on down the street, farting and throwing up dust. The crowd ran into the street following and watching it until it disappeared, heading toward the hills.

For a while after the car had disappeared the people remained, looking toward the dust cloud in the distance, and then they dispersed, talking excitedly. The age of technology had come to San Cristobal.

☠ Raid

My father grew up at a time when there were still frequent battles pitting Indians against settlers and townspeople, and he always felt a distrust of Indians, or "wild" Indians, as he called them—those Indians who did not live or work in town or on one of the ranches. "Tame" Indians were acceptable, but they were also to be watched carefully. When he was fifteen, a friend of his of the same age was hired by a woman who owned a gold mine in the mountains to keep guard over the mine entrance. He was standing guard one day while two Yaqui Indians, "tame" Indians, worked inside the mine. The next time anyone saw his friend, the boy had been disemboweled and his body tied to a pole at the mine entrance. The two "tame" Indians had grabbed and held him while they signaled to some "wild" Indians, who came and killed the boy and took his rifle. And now, years later, Father still warned his children to be wary of Indians and avoid them whenever possible. To reinforce his point, he told us a story about an Indian raid that had occurred when he was a young man of nineteen.

The attack came during the spring roundup when the cattle were brought in and the new calves were branded. As my dad remembered it, most of the men in town were out rounding up the cattle when a band of Yaqui Indians hit the town, wounding a couple of people and killing one, looting some stores, and taking all the horses in the livery stable. It was a quick raid, and within a half an hour they were gone.

When the word got to the men on the range, they hurried home to organize a posse. An officer from a nearby military detachment was in charge, and he quickly picked twelve men to go with him, my father among them. For two days they trailed the Yaquis. At one point, the Indians split into two groups, but the posse stayed together and followed the group with the most horses. The Indians were headed due west, toward the Sea of Cortez between the mainland and the peninsula of Baja California. About one day's ride from the coast, they made contact with the group they were chasing. There was a fight and one of the posse was wounded in the thigh by an arrow, but the posse had managed to capture one of the Indians. The men knew that the Yaquis in that area put poison on their arrow tips, and they were sure that, without an antidote, their man would die. They questioned the captive about an antidote, but the Indian would not talk, even when they threatened to cut off his ears. One of the captors came up to him with an arrow in his hand and jabbed the arrow point hard into the Indian's thigh. The Yaqui fell to the ground and grabbed his leg, trying to staunch the flow of blood. He looked at the men around him and shouted, "*Gorumina! Gorumina!*"

Nobody knew the word or what the Indian meant. "*¡Qué dices, jodido!*" shouted the military officer. What are you saying!

"*Gorumina! Gorumina!*"

The officer reached down and hauled the Indian to his feet. "Show me!" he yelled at him.

The Yaqui limped through the desert shrubs, eagerly looking around. He stopped at a plant the Mexicans call *golondrina* and stripped some of its leaves. He mashed them between his hands and then pressed the crushed leaves against the wound in his thigh. My dad also took a handful of leaves and hurried over to the wounded townsman lying in the shade of a mesquite tree. His wound was turning black and he lay moaning. Father pressed the crushed leaves against the open wound and wrapped a piece of cloth around his leg to hold the leaves in place. The posse decided to leave one man with him to take him to the nearest ranch where he could be tended to. The rest continued the chase, leaving the wounded Indian on foot in the desert to survive or die on his own.

Father remained with the group that continued tracking the raiders. A day later they got to the coast of the Sea of Cortez, where the trail ended on the beach, about twenty miles north of the fishing village of Guaymas. Their frustration and helplessness only made their anger worse. The posse would head back, having accomplished almost nothing.

They had just made the decision to return when three Indians appeared over the dunes at the edge of the sea. They wanted to talk. These were Seri Indians, a handsome warrior people who were traditional enemies of the Yaqui. They said they had spied on the Yaquis from a distance and saw them split into two groups. There were nine Yaquis left. Three of them rode north along the beach, taking all the horses with them. The water had washed away the tracks, and the Seris did not know where the three had taken the horses. (My dad was sure that the Seris had killed these three and taken the horses for their own, but there was simply no way to prove this.) They said the remaining six had taken a large fishing canoe and gone out to sea toward *La Isla del Tiburon* (Shark Island), the sixty-mile-long island barely visible between the mainland and the Baja peninsula. The Yaquis were hiding on Tiburon, the Seris said.

Would the Seris be willing to chase them, the military officer asked. The Mexican government would reward them with food and clothes and tobacco if they caught the Yaquis. The Seris asked for firearms. No firearms, replied the officer.

"Catch them and bring them back with their hands tied, and we will give you blankets, clothes, dry beans and corn, and liquor," offered the officer.

The three talked together in Seri for a few minutes and then said they would get a band of Seris and catch the Yaquis. Within four days, they said, they would be back. "We will have their hands tied," they said.

The posse rode to Guaymas to wait for the Seris to do their job. After four days, a contingent of Seris arrived in Guaymas to talk to the military officer and take their reward. They carried a long pole with them. Tied to the pole were six pairs of hands.

The officer saw that they got their blankets, a bolt of cloth, beans, tobacco, and liquor. A man with a camera was traveling through northern Mexico photographing people and places, and he was in Guaymas when this all happened. At that time, of course, photography was a pretty new thing. He took a picture of the posse and the Seris together, the Seris holding the pole with the hands tied to it. My dad never saw the photograph, but I suppose somewhere in somebody's attic or in a collection of old pictures is a faded photo of the group, including my father. Whoever has the picture probably has no idea what is going on in the photograph.

The posse returned, with no stolen horses, but with the satisfaction of knowing that the Yaquis had paid a heavy price for the horses. The wounded townsman and the man who had stayed with him were picked up on the way back. Eventually, the wounded man recovered completely. My father never knew what became of the Yaqui they had captured and left behind, wounded, in the desert.

♉ El Toro

When I was a child, it was almost impossible to live in Sonora, Mexico, without having direct contact with vaqueros and cattle. It was, after all, Mexicans who invented the cattle industry in the Southwestern United States. You can still see the Mexican connection in the words used by cowboys: *rodeo, lariat, bronco, corral.* My uncle, Rafael Otero, owned a large cattle ranch about a day's ride from San Cristobal, near the town of El Cajon. One spring the whole family went to his ranch and spent about a week there during the cattle roundup and branding. Uncle Rafael needed some temporary hands to help with the roundup, and my father agreed to work with him for a week or so. That week remains one of the clearest memories of my life in Mexico.

Uncle Rafael, a big, red-faced, loud, and friendly man, was married to one of my dad's sisters, by whom he had produced five children—two sons and three daughters. To my seven-year-old eyes, the tall, dark-eyed daughters were the most beautiful girls I had ever seen. For the week we were there, I followed Alicia, the thirteen-year-old, whenever I could. She took me on sort of like a pet, and I had daydreams of growing up, becoming a vaquero, and riding off with her on my dancing black stallion.

My uncle was my godfather since he sponsored me at my baptism. In fact, it was because of my uncle that I was named Rafael. My parents had decided to name me Lorenzo, but at the baptismal font, when the priest asked my godfather for my name, he told him that I was to be named Rafael. Before my astonished parents could react, the priest was baptizing me "Rafael," and Rafael I have remained.

My godfather then gave me a heifer and said he would put my brand on her. Since I was only three days old, I'm not sure just what my "brand" was. Father also had a few head of cattle that a rancher friend let him graze on his range. He added my heifer to this small but growing herd. But like so many other things we had, we left the herd behind when we emigrated to the United States several years later. I suppose my dad's friend wound up with our herd of nine head.

When we arrived at Uncle Rafael's ranch, it was a confusion of noisy activity. Cattle were constantly being brought in from the range, and since the rangeland was not yet fenced in, the different brands from the neighboring ranches were being separated out into herds while the new calves were taken from their mothers and branded. There were vaqueros everywhere, and the noise was constant—men and women joking and laughing, and every now and then a burst of profanity from one of the vaqueros struggling with a stubborn cow. Kids were running around, getting underfoot, arguing, and shouting. And always there was the lowing and complaining of the cattle. A cloud of dust hung in the air around the pens and corrals, and the vaqueros looked ghostly as they wrestled the calves to the ground for branding. A large outdoor stove had been constructed out of adobe blocks on which huge pots of beans and green chile stew were bubbling. There was an open pit over which freshly slaughtered beef was cooking on spits and in which potatoes were roasting in the hot coals. The smells of the cooking food mingled with the smell of fresh manure and the odor of mint, which grew wild along the banks of the irrigation ditches. There was so much mint that when they wanted to divert the flow of water from one ditch to another, they would pull up bundles of mint and use it to block the ditches.

In the evenings everyone gathered around several campfires and ate until no one wanted to move, the exhausted vaqueros often stretching out full length on the ground. There was a lot of oregano that grew wild on Uncle's ranch, and the cattle and deer often grazed on it so that the beef and venison from the ranch came already spiced for cooking over the open fire. After eating, some vaqueros brought out their guitars and the singing began, the *corridos* (the traditional ballads) and the *rancheras* (songs about ranch life), and even songs from the Revolution, then dying a slow and violent death. For many of these people the Revolution had been only a source of anarchy, suffering, and death, but they still found the revolutionary music irresistible. And then the storytelling around the campfires would begin: folktales with a moral; ghost stories to scare the kids; or "true" stories that happened to the teller or the teller's friend, often with a supernatural twist (and often with a number of embellishments stretching the truth just a bit).

For a child, the roundup was heaven.

There was one vaquero in particular, Fermin, who drew the respect of all the other men. People asked him for advice on all sorts of matters and came to him for help with any problem in the roundup. Everybody paid attention when he spoke. He became my ideal vaquero. He was tall and slender with long, perfectly bowed legs, powerful shoulders, and a huge handlebar mustache. And he could ride a horse like no other man. When I wasn't following Alicia around, I was following him. Often I wound up following both at the same time, since Alicia also spent a lot of her free time watching Fermin and being in the same area he was in. This hurt my little love-burdened heart, but I also understood why she felt as she did. In fact, if I had had to choose between Alicia and Fermin, I suppose I would have chosen Fermin.

On the sixth or seventh day of the roundup, there was suddenly a great deal of excitement around one of the corrals. A vaquero had ridden in to announce that El Prieto (the Black One) had been caught and was at that moment being brought in to be branded. El Prieto was a huge, black bull that everyone knew lived on the range, but he had never been brought in to a roundup. He was a completely wild animal that only a few of the vaqueros had ever seen. There was a story that a vaquero once stumbled upon El Prieto on the range, and the bull had gored his horse, knocking it to the ground, crushing the vaquero's leg. That was the closest anyone had come to capturing the wild bull. But now they were bringing him in.

There were three vaqueros handling the one bull. Each had looped a lasso around the bull's neck so that it was being pulled forward and to each side at the same time. I had run out along with everyone else to watch the spectacle. El Prieto had been caught! Even roped and pulled, with sweat pouring off him and wetting the ground beneath, with him gasping for breath, even then he was the most beautiful animal I had ever seen. He was massive and jet-black, and his horns were sharp daggers.

They dragged him into one of the corrals with everyone oohing and ahhing, the men cheering and the women looking a little sad. In the corral, ropes were looped around his legs and he was pulled to the ground, lying on his side. The men holding the ropes kept them taut, preventing El Prieto from getting back up. One of the vaqueros took a saw and cut off his horns, and then another took the red-hot branding iron and pressed it against the bull's flank, burning hair and flesh in a rank cloud of smoke.

I was sitting on the top rail of the corral while this was going on, waiting expectantly for the bull to be let up so that I could see that magnificence standing on its own legs again. But the bull was not let up, the vaqueros keeping the ropes pulled as tight as they could. Then Fermin walked into the corral carrying a five-pound sledgehammer in his hand. He walked to the bull, raised the hammer above his head, and brought it down hard on El Prieto's right hind leg. Even from where I was sitting I could hear the bones breaking as the hammer hit, followed by one of the most terrifying sounds I ever heard as the bull bellowed out his pain and uncomprehending rage.

For a second I almost fell off the fence. My eyes blurred and I was instantly sick to my stomach. Some of the vaqueros cheered and laughed when the leg was broken, as if in some way they had achieved a victory. The ropes around the bull's neck and legs were loosened and removed. After a painful struggle the bull managed to stand up and move slowly toward a corner of the corral, dragging his useless leg behind him.

"There," said Fermin, "he's not so bad anymore."

I jumped off the top rail, turned, and tried to get away from there as fast as I could. I bumped into Alicia, who was standing with her mouth wide in horror. I ran to one of the empty irrigation ditches and hid in it so no one could see me while I cried. I decided then that I would not become a vaquero.

That night there were the usual gatherings around the campfires, the joking and storytelling, and the singing. From one fire I heard a low, sad voice singing a verse from an old corrido:

> *Bajáron al toro prieto*
> *Que nunca lo habían bajado,*
> *Pero ahora si ya bajó,*
> *Revuelto con el ganado.*

> (They have brought down the big black bull,
> The one they've never brought down before,
> But now they've brought him down
> Mixed in with all the other cattle.)

The next day the roundup was over, and everyone began heading home to recuperate from the feverish activity that had been going on for over a week.

My family was packed and ready to head back to San Cristobal. As we left Uncle's ranch, I waved goodbye to Alicia, who was standing alone by one of the cattle pens, looking at the big black bull slumped against the rails of the corral, with his head hanging down, eyes glazed, spittle stringing down from his mouth. I don't believe she saw me.

43

☾ A Wake

idelio Padilla was thirty years old when he died, of a heart attack most people said. But since San Cristobal was a small, quiet Mexican town, for some people the factual and commonplace were not exciting enough. These people nodded knowingly and implied that they could, if they wanted, reveal certain "unnatural" facts about his death that would make the whole town shudder. They glanced about nervously while they talked, as if someone were just around the corner eavesdropping. The leader of this group was Doña Luisa, an ancient crone who dressed all in black in honor of her deceased husband, who had passed away seventeen years earlier.

"She *should* dress in black," said Ramon Padilla, Fidelio's father, when he heard the rumors about his son's death. "She spends all her time in church reciting the rosary, but her heart is as black as her skirts! It was living with her for thirty-seven years that drove her husband to his death."

The truth is that Ramon never did get along with Fidelio, his only child. Ramon and his wife, Josefa, lived in the same house with their son until he was about twenty, when he moved into a shack behind the house.

But even when they lived in the same house, father and son rarely talked to each other.

My dad told me that when Josefa was pregnant with Fidelio, Ramon got drunk and accused Doña Luisa of being a witch, and supposedly she cursed him and his offspring. About four months later, Fidelio was born a hunchback, and two years after that, Josefa started going blind. Ramon believed that Doña Luisa was the cause of his son's deformity and his wife's blindness, and he developed a powerful hatred of her. Only his fear of her kept him from retaliating, and his anger smoldered hotly inside him. Meanwhile, it was clear to us that Ramon could barely stand the sight of his hunchbacked son.

Fidelio was about five feet tall, and the hump on his back was so big that when he walked he seemed to be bent way over from its crushing weight, even when he was standing perfectly straight. To me, he looked like a grotesque ape when I saw him walking down the street from a distance. I guess it was his strange appearance that made some people in town associate him with evil forces. "When he goes into the desert and spends all day there, he and the devil come up with plots against the good people of San Cristobal," a few people said. I was familiar with the rumors and was scared to be anywhere near him. But most people in town pretty much accepted his presence in the community. My dad always got angry whenever he heard people talk about Fidelio as evil. *Mitoteros*, he called them, rumor-spreading witches. Still, I made a point to avoid Fidelio whenever I saw him. However, when I was nine, my friend Enrique changed my feelings about Fidelio.

Enrique was three years older than I was. I had become friends with him because I used to play with his younger brother Chencho, who was my age. Enrique was very quiet and seemed to know more about more things than any other kid in San Cristobal. Like Fidelio, Enrique spent a lot of time by himself, often spending all day in the desert or the nearby hills and not returning until after dark. During one of these excursions (he told me later), he encountered Fidelio, and the two spent the afternoon talking. I guess you could say they became friends, or at least Enrique was the closest thing to a friend that Fidelio had.

One day Enrique and I were in town when I saw Fidelio walking toward us. I grabbed Enrique's arm and said, "Quick, let's cross the street!"

Enrique snorted at me in disgust. "You're acting just like that old witch Doña Luisa and her friends. Fidelio's a good guy."

Although I was scared I stood my ground, standing next to Enrique, who greeted Fidelio warmly. Fidelio looked closely at me while he spoke to Enrique. "Come see me this afternoon," he said. "I have something to show you." Then he walked on.

Enrique looked at me and laughed. "I tell you, Fidelio is a good guy, better than most people in this town." He put his hand on my shoulder. "Listen, I'm going to see Fidelio later today. I'll stop by and take you with me."

I wanted to tell him that I would rather not go, but I wanted his respect, so I agreed to meet him later.

In mid-afternoon Enrique came for me, and we walked over to the Padillas', out toward the river, about a half-mile from the edge of town. When we got to the house, Enrique called out Fidelio's name loudly.

"I'm back here," Fidelio shouted from the backyard.

We walked around the house. He was sitting under a cottonwood tree, whittling. He barely glanced at me.

"Look," he said to Enrique as he reached for a wooden box beside him. He pulled a woodcarving from the box and gave it to Enrique, who handled it gently, turning it over in his hands several times.

"Here," said Enrique, handing it to me. It was a bird, a roadrunner, carved with his head thrust forward and his wings just beginning to spread. There were all these details in the carving: ridged feathers, the plume on its head, its tiny eyes, slightly open beak, and even the scales on its feet. It was beautiful.

"Did you carve this?" I stammered.

"Of course he did," said Enrique. "Fidelio is the best wood-carver in Mexico. But nobody knows it." He took the carving back from me as if he were a priest handling the communion host at mass. He placed it carefully back in the box and lifted another carving out of it and handed it to me. "Look at this one," he said.

It was a *santo*, a carving of a saint, standing straight and looking into my eyes with a disturbing expression on its face. I could see wounds on his hands and bare feet, which told me it was Saint Francis. He had a little bird perched on his shoulder and a rabbit looking up at him from the carving's base. I knew as I held it that this was something holy. Fidelio was watching me closely and smiled as I gave it to him. I had never seen him smile before.

We spent about an hour with Fidelio, long enough to see the other carvings in the box and some that he brought out from his shack. There were carvings of desert wildlife and religious statues, including one of Jesus on the cross that was so full of suffering it was painful to look at, in a strange-good sort of way.

As we walked back to town, Enrique asked me if I still thought of Fidelio as a friend of the devil.

"Why does Doña Luisa say those things about him?" I asked.

Enrique burst out laughing. "This morning you were acting toward him the same way she does! He's different, and she's a *mitotera* who tries to put down anybody who's better than she is. And she likes to make his father angry."

"Why doesn't he show everybody his carvings? Then people like Doña Luisa would stop saying bad things about him. And he could probably sell them for lots of money."

"If Doña Luisa saw the carvings she would probably accuse Fidelio of using them for witchcraft. The old witch! And he doesn't want or need any more money than he already has."

"Then why does he carve them if nobody sees them?"

"I see them," said Enrique, "and now you see them too. I know how good they are, and you do too. I think that's enough for Fidelio."

I returned with Enrique to see Fidelio one more time, about a week later, and he showed us a carving he was working on. It was a hawk, and he had finished the head when we saw it. The hawk had the same powerful eyes as the Saint Francis I had seen the first time. We visited with him for a while and then headed home.

Several days later Fidelio died.

I was so upset when I heard the news from Enrique that I got sick to my stomach. Now nobody would know what Fidelio was really like, and there would be no more of the magical carvings. He died in his sleep, Enrique said, probably the way he wanted to die. And almost immediately, Doña Luisa started her foul rumors about witchcraft and black magic.

Preparations for the wake, which was to be held that evening (in warm climates people must act quickly in these matters), began almost immediately. A Mexican wake is more than just people showing up to pay their respects to the deceased and to express their sympathies to the living; it is also an occasion for feasting and drinking and remembering the good times the departed one supposedly shared with those left living. Of course, only Enrique would have such memories of Fidelio, but the rest of the town did not let that stop them, and people made up memories when necessary.

That afternoon I went with Enrique to see Josefa, Fidelio's mother. She immediately recognized Enrique's footsteps and greeted him warmly. "You were Fidelio's only true friend," she said, crying and holding him.

Enrique introduced me and told her that I too had become his friend just before his death. She reached for me blindly and hugged me. "He was such a good boy," she sobbed. "Only you know how good he really was. My poor boy suffered so much, and now there he lies in the bed. Fidelio!" she wailed. "At least now you will be with Jesus, and no one will hurt you again."

We looked through the open door to the bedroom where Fidelio's corpse had been laid out. His father, Ramon, and another townsman were standing on either side of the bed. Ramon handed a rope to his companion. While we watched, they ran the rope across Fidelio's chest and under the bed, and then each man took an end of the rope and pulled as hard he could. The harder they pulled, the more pressure the rope exerted on Fidelio's chest, forcing his upper torso back, pivoting on his hump until his head and neck were resting on the pillow.

Ramon looked up and saw the two of us watching them. "His Goddamn hump is so big he can't lie flat on the bed," he explained. "Instead of lying down, he was sitting up. We can't have that at a wake." They tied the two ends underneath the bed and then covered the body with a sheet up to the neck. Then they stood back and admired the results of their labor. Fidelio was lying as flat on his back as is possible for a hunchback.

On the way back to town Enrique suddenly erupted in a string of profanity. "That rotten no good sonuvabitch! *¡Cabrón! ¡Hijo de puta!* All he ever saw when Fidelio was alive was his hump. And now that his son is dead, that's still all he's concerned about. The bastard! I'll teach him about humps!" He said nothing the rest of the way home.

That night most of the people in town went to Fidelio's wake, even those who had whispered behind his back when he had been alive. For the most part, the men remained outside in the yard, talking and passing around bottles of beer and tequila. Every now and then, one or two of them would feel obligated to pay their respects to the deceased, so they would go into the bedroom, cross themselves, mumble a few words, and then go back out to the circulating bottles of tequila. When we got there, Ramon Padilla was already quite drunk. Most of the women were in the house, in the kitchen ladling out bowls of *menudo* or beans and piling steaming tamales onto trays. The women, too, would wander into the bedroom to say a prayer or two, or they would kneel together in the living room reciting the rosary with Josefa. The truly pious, such as Doña Luisa and her followers, would stay in the bedroom all night, imploring for the soul of the departed. I was glad to see that Doña Luisa, who always attended wakes and funerals, had not yet arrived.

I played for a few minutes with the other kids in the yard until Enrique showed up. He motioned to me, and we went into the bedroom together to pay our last respects. Fidelio was still lying there, twisted backward over his hump, covered by a sheet. Enrique and I knelt down by the bedside and prayed quietly.

There was a sudden commotion outside that we could hear clearly through the open window of the bedroom. I could hear Ramon shouting something, with other people joining in, and then the soft voices of the peacemakers interrupted by hoarse screams from Ramon. "I don't want that witch in my house! She's the one who cursed me and my poor son!" More sobs and moans. The commotion moved indoors, and there was Doña Luisa making her appearance in the doorway of the bedroom. People began moving aside to make room for her as she knelt at the foot of the bed and began a loud prayer for Fidelio's soul.

"O Most Powerful Father who loves all his children, even his wicked and deformed ones, please pour all your love and grace on us, unworthy sinners though we be, and especially give your grace and love to this wicked son of sin who comes before your throne to be judged."

Enrique jabbed me in the ribs with his elbow. I glanced over at him. He had pulled out a pocketknife and was slowly sawing at the rope that held poor Fidelio's corpse down.

Doña Luisa was really getting into her prayer now, her voice increasing in volume as she went on. "Dear Father, please give this unworthy sinner the joy of eternal life, even though he does not deserve your mercy and your love! GIVE HIM ETERNAL LIFE AND

LET HIM LIVE FOREVER AMONG YOUR SAINTS. . . ." Her voice was thundering now.

What happened next is kind of jumbled in my memory. On one side of me was Doña Luisa rumbling, on the other side was Enrique and his knife. I heard a *twang!* and Fidelio's corpse suddenly sprang up into a sitting position, the sheet flying off of him, his arms cast forward by the energy released by the cut rope. He balanced for a moment, rocking backward a little, and then forward, until he settled, bent at the waist with his hands resting on his knees. Somebody screamed. I turned to see Doña Luisa's eyes roll back in her head as she keeled over in a dead faint. Now everyone was screaming. People were trying to get out the bedroom door at the same time, but two or three had gotten stuck in the doorway and were elbowing each other and yelling. Others were clambering out the open window, tumbling into the dirt and crawling away. I got roughly pushed out of the way and wound up half under the bed.

All at once the bedroom was completely still and all the commotion and screaming were outside. Enrique pulled me out from under the bed.

"We'd better go," he whispered. He paused at the doorway, looked back at the sitting Fidelio, and winked. Doña Luisa was coming to and sat up dazed. She took one look at Fidelio, who seemed to be looking right at her, gave a low moan, and keeled over again. We left, walking calmly out into the middle of the storm.

When we got to Enrique's house we stopped at the gate and started laughing. We were rolling on the ground. "Did you see . . . ? What about . . . ? Did you hear what . . . ?" We lay on the ground gasping for breath.

"Fidelio," said Enrique. "That was for you. O God, God! I hope you saw it all, my friend."

The next morning Fidelio's wake was on everyone's lips. People were gathered in small groups whispering outside the church before Fidelio's funeral mass. Those who had bruises from their hurried escape from the room in which Fidelio had lain were making jokes about others climbing out the window or squeezing through the door. Despite Mother's attempts to keep her brood together, we kids all scattered throughout the church-yard listening to the gossip.

"There was a flash," said Bernabo to his enthralled listeners, "and a loud noise like a railroad train, and Fidelio was standing up in his bed with his eyes wide and glowing bright red! I was there, I saw it with these two eyes."

"I myself saw a huge figure in a black cloak appear by the bed," asserted Elisa Romero, "but he was there for only a second or two, his head touching the ceiling, his arms spread wide, from wall to wall."

"I was standing outside, by the window," said another, "and I could smell burning sulfur when Fidelio howled and sat up."

"I saw a shape with hooves and a tail," said Enrique, "and it was bending over and helping Doña Luisa sit up after she had fainted. She looked grateful."

At this comment, those who heard Enrique looked a little confused, not sure what to make of this bit of information.

Enrique and I did not go to the funeral mass. I would have some explaining to do to my mother, but I went with Enrique to Fidelio's shack. We went in. Enrique got down on his hands and knees, reached under

Fidelio's bed, and pulled out two boxes. They were full of carvings.

Without saying a word, we took the boxes, along with Fidelio's carving tools, and went to the foothills outside of town. We gathered a large bundle of dead chamisa, piled it over the two boxes of tools and carvings, and lit it.

We sat on the ground and watched the flames until there was nothing left but ashes and the blackened steel of his tools. We scattered the ashes with our feet and then walked silently back to town.

 El Chapo

One of the most exciting social events in the life of San Cristobal was the Great Race in which Fermino Réal ran his horse, El Guapo, against the bay from Canitullo. The whole town was buzzing about it days before the race. El Guapo had never lost a race and was well known in all the ranches and villages around San Cristobal. But even so, the rumor was going round that the bay was faster than El Guapo. Bets were being made by virtually everyone in town and the surrounding area, and there were many arguments and even a fistfight or two over who would win the race.

A couple of days before the race, people started showing up in wagons, setting up tents outside of town and booths in the central plaza from which to sell food, drinks, huaraches, pants, shirts, blankets, and even saddles. The race had become a giant fair.

I was in my dad's cantina/pool hall listening to the talk of the race, when Chapo Miguel ("Short Mike") came in. It was only about ten o'clock in the morning, but he was already drunk. He was obnoxious and aggressive when he was sober, and became more so whenever he was drunk. As usual, he was boasting about something. He claimed to have seen both horses race, and that only a fool would bet against the bay. Somehow this simple idea got confused with his manhood. He offered to fight any son of a bitch that disagreed with his opinion of the race.

"Come on, you cowards!" he slobbered. "Anyone here think I don't know what I'm talking about? Well, let's step outside and we'll see who the real man in this town is. I'm more macho than any ten of you put together."

The men in San Cristobal were familiar with Chapo and generally ignored his threats and boasts, so they continued talking and drinking as if Chapo weren't there. Being ignored only increased his anger, and he actually began pushing one of the men standing at the bar. Father immediately came from behind the bar, hustled Chapo out onto the street, and told him not to return until he had calmed down. He staggered down the street shouting threats at my dad, who turned and walked back into his cantina.

The next day, the day before the race, Chapo came into the cantina pretty much sober, but quite excited about something. He said that he had just heard that Juan Rojo, a bitter enemy of his (at least from Chapo's point of view), was coming into town for the race.

"Gimme a tequila," he ordered. "At last that coward is coming back to town. Now, he'll have to face me. He won't have a chance to hide." He gulped down his tequila.

The year before, Rojo had come to San Cristobal to buy a horse. He was having a drink in the cantina when Chapo showed up and started pestering him. Chapo kept pressuring him to fight, but Rojo hardly knew him and kept trying to calm the man down. But each attempt to back off only drew more insults from Chapo. Finally the two of them stepped out into the street. Chapo took one swing and missed. Rojo grabbed him, spun him around, and tripped him to the ground on his face. Pressing Chapo down with his knee against Chapo's back and pinning him to the ground, Rojo then pulled Chapo's pants down around his ankles. He stood up and walked away. Chapo, more enraged than ever, scrambled to his feet and tried to run after Rojo, but his pants immediately tripped him flat in the middle of the street. By now a sizeable crowd was watching and laughing. Chapo sat up, trying drunkenly to pull his pants up while Juan Rojo continued his leisurely stroll down Main Street. When Chapo finally did get his pants above his knees, he stood up only to have the pants fall down again. The crowd was roaring. When he bent down to grab at his pants, he lost his balance and fell face forward again. By the time he had his pants up around his waist, Juan Rojo was no longer in sight.

This humiliation had festered in Chapo's soul for the past year. And now at last the time of retribution was at hand. He drank another tequila and began shouting about what he was going to do to Juan Rojo. Everyone ignored him.

The morning of the race Chapo was going up and down Main Street looking for the magistrate, who happened to be my father. He finally tracked Father down in the office of the comisario.

"I have some business with the magistrate," said Chapo.

"All right," said Father, opening the magistrate's drawer of his desk. "What do you need?"

"I want to know how much you would fine someone for punching another person in public."

"Fighting in public is against the law, and if you do so, I will throw you in jail."

"No, no," said Chapo. "I didn't say anything about fighting. I mean just one punch, no *fighting*. If I should just happen to accidentally punch someone in the nose, how much fine would I have to pay?"

"One punch without fighting?" Father asked dubiously. "I've never heard of anything like that. I guess I would fine you ten pesos."

Chapo reached into his pocket and pulled out a ten-peso note. "Here." He handed the ten to Father. "Now, if I should happen to punch someone, I've got my fine covered, and there will be no need for you to arrest me." He turned and walked out of the office before Father could say anything.

The story of the fine spread quickly through the streets. When people saw Chapo walking around asking if anyone had seen Juan Rojo, everyone knew what was happening. A friend of Rojo's asked why this character was going around looking for him. When he learned the cause, he laughed and said his compadre Juan could take care of himself. But he went looking for him anyway, to give him fair warning.

Once Rojo heard what was happening, he, in turn, started searching for Chapo. He found him in the middle of the street, with his back to Rojo, talking to another man. Rojo tapped him on the shoulder.

"*Oyé cabrón*, I hear you're looking for me." Rojo then hauled back and punched Chapo square on the nose, flattening him on the street, unconscious.

My dad, who was also something like a sergeant-at-arms—the closest thing to a police force in San Cristobal—promptly arrested Rojo for fighting in public, and took him to his office, where he became the magistrate. Sitting at his desk across from Rojo, Father reviewed the case with the little office packed with bystanders, while those who couldn't fit indoors listened through the open window. Chapo, who had been revived with a bucket of water, was also in attendance, holding a handkerchief to his bloody nose.

"There is a law against fighting in public in San Cristobal," he told the defendant.

"But we didn't fight," answered Rojo. "I just threw one punch and the other guy didn't throw any."

Father turned to Chapo. "Did you throw a punch?" he asked.

"No!" screamed Chapo. "This *jodido* punched me when I wasn't looking. I didn't have the chance to fight."

"So there was no fight," said Father. "Well, we decided earlier that if there was only one punch thrown, that was not a fight, and there would be a ten-peso fine for the one punch. So we fine you ten pesos for the punch."

Juan Rojo was reaching into his pocket for his bill-fold when Father interrupted him.

"Wait," he said. "There are other circumstances to consider. Earlier today Chapo paid a ten-peso fine just in case somebody happened to punch someone else but there was no fight. Well, of all the strange coincidences one can imagine, such an event has actually happened: there has been one punch thrown with no fight. Chapo, with an admirable sense of civic duty and generosity, has already paid the fine for the punch, so there is no need for the defendant to pay another fine. Case dismissed. Now, will everyone clear out of my office so we can go see the race?"

The crowd moved out and down the street, hooting and laughing at the court's decision, while Chapo stood dumbfounded for a moment, and then followed the crowd, screaming his outrage. No one paid him any attention.

Lazarus

Lazaríllo Madero was a big man. Seen through the eyes of my childhood, he was a giant: tall, broad-shouldered, with a chest that thrust out and strained the buttons on his shirt, and huge, calloused hands. I would watch him arm-wrestle all comers in the cantina, and never did I see anyone even come close to beating him. But like many big men, he was quiet and gentle. He came to San Cristobal from Cananea, to the north of us, where he had worked in the copper mines. He bought a ranch about six or seven miles from town. He hired two hands and together they had run a herd of cattle on the ranch for six years. He smiled a lot and was quite shy until he had a few shots of tequila, and then he became talkative and made up for his usual silence. Even then, however, he was never violent or aggressive.

All the townspeople knew about him was what he revealed about himself during those rare periods when he came into town and had his few drinks. He told us that in Cananea once he and another miner were setting some dynamite when it exploded prematurely. The blast blew his companion to bits, but for Lazaríllo, the explosion only singed his eyebrows off, disintegrated his shirt, and threw him back violently on the ground. Other than

The Horse in the Kitchen

that, and a few days of deafness, he was unharmed. He
told the story and laughed. "My good father up above
must have been watching over me. I don't know why me
and not my *compadre*."

Another time he just missed being caught in a cave-
in in one of the mineshafts. He and a co-worker were
pushing a cart full of ore toward the mine exit when the
ground started shaking and rumbling. The two of them
left the cart and ran to the exit just as the ceiling collapsed behind them. Nine men died in the accident. All
Lazaríllo got was a bruise from a rock that had struck his
thigh. "Thanks be to Jesus for taking care of me," he said.

On his own ranch, he was rounding up strays on the
high range one day in early March. He was on horseback
chasing a cow and her heifer when his horse stepped in
a prairie dog hole and fell, rolling its full weight on
Lazaríllo. Both the horse and rider suffered a broken leg.
The horse managed to move off Lazaríllo, but then it lay
on its side whinnying in pain. Lazaríllo crawled the few
feet to the suffering animal, pulled his 30-30 from its
scabbard, and shot the horse.

It was afternoon and the weather was turning ugly.
Soon the wind was blowing hard as a late winter storm
moved in. At first, he lay by the horse, using its body to
protect himself from the wind, but as the sun lowered,
the temperature dropped below freezing. He realized he
would freeze to death lying there in the open, so he took
his knife, and lying on his side, managed to slice open
the horse's abdomen and gut it. He then crawled into the
horse's body cavity and lay on his back with most of his
broken left leg sticking out. He spent the night half-
delirious with pain, but he survived. The next morning
only the toes on his left leg were frostbitten.

Slowly and painfully, he crawled out from the horse. The storm was gone and the sun had risen over the ridge. He lay for a while, trying to absorb the little heat the sun was putting out. He knew that his two hired hands would soon be looking for him, so after waiting for an hour or so, he took his rifle and fired one shot into the air. Then he waited some more. He fired again, and again he waited. He had two rounds left in his 30-30. He fired once more, and a minute later he heard an answering shot in the distance. He lay for a while, and then fired his last round. This time the answering shot was considerably closer. After a few minutes of waiting, he heard shouts. He called back, and a short while later the two hired men rode over the ridge. Lazaríllo, lying there encrusted with the dried gore from the horse, explained what had happened. They gave him several shots of tequila, put a splint on his leg, and then set him on a horse behind one of them. Lazaríllo and the hand were roped together so he wouldn't fall off. In this manner they got him back to the ranch where he pretty much recovered, except that he lost two toes and walked with a limp from then on. "I guess God and my poor horse were watching over me that time, too," he said.

To me, Lazaríllo was indestructible. He told his stories, and I would listen in open-mouthed admiration. He was everything I thought a man should be. He never boasted; he just told his tales in a matter-of-fact way, as if any man could have undergone his ordeals. This was true manhood, and nothing could destroy it. I guess he knew how I felt about him because whenever he came to town he would make a point to greet me and shake my hand.

One day one of his hired hands rode into town to tell us that Lazaríllo had come down with an illness after returning from a trip to Cananea to visit some friends. He said it was some kind of skin disease or rash, and that Lazaríllo's fingers were the same gray color his toes had been with the frostbite. There was no doctor in San Cristobal, but Refugio, who ran the livery stable, knew quite a bit of veterinary medicine from practical experience. So he went to check on Lazaríllo. When he came back, he looked grim. Lazaríllo, he told us, had leprosy.

The news sent a wave of fear through the entire town. It was clear that Lazaríllo would have to be sent away to a leper colony. A delegation rode to his ranch to make the arrangements to move him out. They came back hours later and, with people gathered in the main street, they explained what had occurred with Lazaríllo. He had pleaded with them not to send him off to a colony to die. They had argued that surely he could see that he was threatening the entire community if he remained. He had gotten on his knees and wept. To see this strong man so desperate that he cried like a baby was a real shock to the delegation. He told them he would kill himself before he went to a leper colony. Eventually they came to an agreement. The townspeople would build him a shack at the base of the sierra about five miles from town, and he would live there and never leave the premises. If he failed to live up to this agreement, they would send him to a colony. Once a week the town would provide him with food and water and give him some human companionship—at a distance, of course. Lazaríllo told them he had no family, so the delegation agreed to oversee the running of his ranch and to make sure the hired hands were paid out of whatever money the ranch made. Any money leftover would be used to pay for food and supplies for him.

And so it happened. Every Monday, a considerable portion of the community would make the five-mile trip to his shack and unload a couple of barrels of water and a supply of flour and other foodstuffs. Everyone would stand about thirty feet from him while he asked questions about his ranch and life in town. After an hour or so, we would all leave and head back to town. I would keep looking back, seeing him standing there watching the departing townspeople until he was nothing more than a speck in the far distance.

This system worked all right for the first three or four weeks, but then something happened and the system broke down. Don Fermino Réal was going to race his horse, El Guapo, against a horse from Canitullo, and the winner would take the loser's horse. The race was the most exciting event that had happened in San Cristobal in years. People from all the surrounding communities were arriving in San Cristobal several days in advance, and the whole event became a giant fair.

In all the excitement and preparations for the race, everyone forgot about Lazaríllo in his lonely shack at the foot of the sierra. That Monday there were no supplies delivered and no chance for Lazaríllo to have the local gossip and news. The race was run toward the end of the week (Don Fermino won the race and the bay from Canitullo), and then there was a collective sigh of relief as the crowds left and the town returned to normal. The following Monday people remembered Lazaríllo again, and everyone became guiltily aware that his supplies had not been delivered for two weeks. Water and food were hastily loaded onto a wagon and a large crowd rode out to the sierra to apologize to the poor leper.

As the crowd approached the shack, Lazaríllo stepped out and waved. He expressed some irritation at having been so quickly forgotten, but he also smiled happily.

"My fingers and toes are healing!" he shouted.

People in the crowd looked around at each other and shook their heads sadly. Poor Lazaríllo had not really accepted the fact of his leprosy. But no one said anything in disagreement. Then we noticed that his face, particularly his nose, did not have that gray, decaying look that it had had two weeks earlier.

"It's true!" shouted Lazaríllo. "Look! See my hands? The fingers have new skin, fresh skin!" He held his hands out in front of him, turning them so we could see both sides. They looked healthy and whole. He started moving toward them, but the crowd backed up hurriedly, so he stopped. "I'm almost cured!" he shouted again.

"How can you be cured?" asked one of the townspeople. "Everyone knows leprosy cannot be cured."

"I don't give a damn what everybody knows! My body is healing!"

Lazaríllo explained that the day after we had last delivered supplies there had been a heavy rain that had filled a barrel with the runoff from the roof of his shed. A day or two later, he had drunk a sip of the water and liked the taste of it better than the taste of the water we had brought him, so he had been drinking that water ever since. He said that a few days after he started drinking the rainwater, he started feeling better, and after about a week he could see that his body was regenerating.

"You wait and see," he shouted, "next week I'll be going back to my ranch, complete and whole."

People couldn't believe that anyone could defeat leprosy, but there he was with what looked like fresh, pink skin on his hands and face. Everybody went home, confused by what they had been told and what they had seen. There was some talk of a miracle in progress, but everybody was still cautious. Perhaps it was nothing more than wishful thinking on everyone's part.

The next Monday, practically the entire town rode out to the base of the sierra to see Lazaríllo. He met everyone standing with his legs spread, hands on hips, and a giant grin on his face. There was no sign of leprosy that anyone could see. Most of the women and some of the men immediately fell to their knees and started praying. "*¡Un milagro! ¡Bendito séa Dios!*"

Lazaríllo boomed out a laugh. "My father God is still watching over me! Look! Look! I'm whole again!"

The agnostics and atheists in the group were the most confused of all. Slowly they walked up closer and closer to Lazaríllo until they could reach out and touch him. They could still see no signs of leprosy.

"The water!" shouted a woman. "God has blessed the water in the rain barrel!"

Suddenly everyone was running toward the barrel. The first ones to reach it scooped out handfuls and splashed it in their faces, drinking mouthfuls and rubbing it against their skin, while those behind pushed them out of the way. Someone ran into the shed and came out with a pan that he filled with the water after ruthlessly pushing his way in. People were crying and laughing, shouting Hosannas to the sky. The barrel was almost empty, so they turned it over to get the last drop of miracle water. Something fell out of the barrel onto the ground. Those around the barrel stopped and were quiet. Lying on the ground was the almost completely decayed corpse and the skeleton of a rattlesnake.

For weeks afterward, a debate raged in San Cristobal between those who said the water was blessed by God and those who said the rattlesnake was the cause of the healing. In the cantina, in the churchyard, on the streets, and in the stores people were shouting and pointing fingers at one another. There were even a few who came to blows over the rattlesnake/God controversy. Some friendships were destroyed forever, and years later there were still people who had little bottles of miracle water that they kept in special altars they set up in their homes.

Lazaríllo went back to his ranch, but he seemed to feel that he had used up the last of his special protection from God. He became much more cautious, and not too long after, he sold his ranch and moved to Hermosillo. The last we heard, he was married and had a family and a quite successful business installing water closets for homes in the city.

Mexican Horses
Part I

For a Mexican man, *un macho*, a horse was more than just an animal. He was *familia*, a child, a boon companion, and best friend, and in the desert a good horse could make the difference between life and death. A man and his horse were like a lover and his sweetheart: for his horse he would do just about anything, even go against his own beliefs and principles.

When I was nine years old, there was a rancher, Fermino Réal, who was a true gambler and would bet on anything. He would bet on which of two birds in a tree would be the first to fly; or whether the morning train would be early, late, or on time; or which drop of rain sliding down a window pane would be the first to reach the bottom of the glass. He had a big chestnut stallion, El Guapo he called him, and he was the fastest horse around. Don Fermino would challenge anyone proud of his own horse to a race, and he never lost, not once. The people from that area soon knew never to challenge Don Fermino and his chestnut to a race. El Guapo was the most beautiful creature I had ever seen. He was strong and delicate at the same time, with long legs that should have been too slender to support the weight of any rider, but those same legs made it seem like he was flying when at full gallop.

I knew that horse as well as I knew my own face. I used to dream that he was mine and I was galloping across the fields with all the other men and horses in my dust, my hair blowing back as I flew above the ground. Everyone was cheering, wondering who the daring horseman with the angelic horse was. How that horse could run!

Then we started hearing rumors about another horse, a bay that a man in Canitullo had, about two days' ride from our village. People were saying that this horse was beating all horses for miles around, and that he was so fast he could outrun El Guapo. Don Fermino took that as a personal insult. He boarded the train to Canitullo, spoke to the bay's owner, and arranged a race between the two horses at our village in three weeks. He came back beaming. They had not only arranged for a race, but what they had agreed to as the prize for the winner left everyone in our town buzzing with excitement: whoever won the race would keep the other's horse as the prize.

The closer the day of the race, the more excited the people became. Most of the townspeople were convinced that Don Fermino's chestnut would win and were betting heavily on him. Don Fermino himself had no doubt. He strutted about town joking and laughing about the new horse he was going to get or sat in the cantina accepting people's congratulations and drinking round after round to his unbeatable horse.

When the race day finally came there were people from miles around. It was like the feast of St. Christopher, the town's patron saint. There were food vendors, lots of tequila, loud boasting and betting, and plenty of fist fights. Don Fermino was still laughing and slapping people on the back, but to me he seemed nervous and worried. Of course the owner of the bay was there too, but he seemed calm and sure.

The race was to begin at one end of Main Street. Each horse was to be ridden by one of the owner's ranch hands. The horses would run the length of the street through town, stay on the road for about a quarter of a mile, then cut off and head toward the river on the trail that led to the Lopez Ranch, run parallel to the river for over a half-mile, then head back to the main road, and finally down the main road back to town and the starting line, which was also the finish line. The course was about two miles long.

When the race started, people were lined up along Main Street from one end of town to the other while others were sitting on the roofs of stores and houses. I was standing on a hitching rail, holding on to one of the posts that supported the roof over the sidewalk in front of the cantina, right at the finish line. The race started, the horses galloping down the street through town. By the time they got to the other end of the main street, they were running neck and neck, and then they continued on in a cloud of dust and were lost from sight.

For those with large bets, the next few moments dragged on and on. Nobody could tell what was happening, and the excitement was intense. Then some of those on the roofs started shouting, "Here they come!" But the cloud of dust the horses were kicking up made it impossible to tell who was ahead. People on the street were craning their necks and straining their eyes. Then from the roofs came the cry, "It's the chestnut!" And sure enough, running across the finish line about ten feet ahead of the bay was El Guapo.

Then something strange happened. Instead of stopping after crossing the finish line, the rider kept the horse running down the main street, all the way to the end of town where horse and rider turned sharply to the right and disappeared behind the livery stable, the last building in town. The bay, however, had stopped shortly after crossing the finish line.

Everyone was puzzled, wondering why the rider had not stopped, but a few seconds later, horse and rider reappeared around the corner of the building and headed back toward the finish line. By now people were massed in the street, the winners laughing and demanding payment on their bets, the losers grumbling. People were slapping Don Fermino on the back, pushing him into the closest cantina for a victory drink. His horse and its rider were stalled in the middle of the street.

I've said I knew that horse as well as I knew my own face, and when the winner crossed the finish line, I noticed there was a white spot on the inside of the left foreleg, just below where it joined the body. I was very confused since I had never noticed that spot on El Guapo before. I was in the street near the horse, so I ducked down to get a better look at that foreleg. There was no white spot on the foreleg. I then knew for sure that this was not the horse that had just run the race.

Without thinking I started shouting, "That's not the same horse that ran the race! This is a different horse!" But since I was just a kid, nobody paid any particular attention to me. I was about to grab the sleeve of the man next to me and shout again, when he grabbed me, placed his hand over my mouth, and dragged me back into an alley off the main street. It was Luis, Don Fermino's foreman.

"Shut up!" he said. He told me if I said anything about the horse, he would cut my tongue out and I would never tell anyone anything again. Of course I was terrified, so I nodded agreement and he took his hand off my mouth. After that scare, I did not feel like joining the celebration of the local folks, so I went on home.

I thought about the race for a few days, wondering what had happened but still too worried about Luis's threat to talk to anyone about it. Three or four days later I was walking down Main Street when I heard someone calling.

"¡Oyé muchacho! ¡Ven aqui!"

I turned and saw Don Fermino standing by the cantina door, gesturing at me to come over. I was a little scared, but I walked over to him.

"Luis told me about you," he said. "Have you talked to anyone about the race?"

"No Señor."

"Good boy." Don Fermino looked around quickly, and then said, "Come with me."

He stepped into the alley next to the cantina with me following him. Watching him stumble into the alley I realized that Don Fermino was tipsy. He stopped and squatted on his haunches, leaning against the wall.

"Let me tell you what happened with the race," he began. "Ay muchacho, you must never tell anyone what I am going to say, or my reputation will be ruined in this town. Do you promise that?"

I agreed, and Don Fermino told his tale.

Don Fermino thought he had complete confidence in his chestnut, but about ten days before the race a friend had come to Don Fermino's house to tell him that he had seen the bay in Canitullo run a race, and in his opinion, the bay was faster than El Guapo. At first, Don Fermino refused to believe this, but when another man told him the same thing, he got very worried. The idea of losing his chestnut was more than he could bear. So he went from almost total confidence to being convinced that he was going to lose. He started having nightmares about the race.

About five days before the race, Don Fermino was in the cantina trying to relieve his fears when a stranger who was passing through came in for a drink while waiting for the train to leave. He began asking for the owner of the chestnut hitched to the rail outside. When Don Fermino spoke up, the man asked him how he had managed to get his horse here from Las Lomas so quickly, since Las Lomas was a two days' train ride away, and the stranger had seen the chestnut there just the day before yesterday.

When Don Fermino explained that his horse had not left the area for days, the stranger expressed amazement. He told Fermino that his horse had an exact twin in Las Lomas. He said that he had paid particular attention to the horse since it was one of the most beautiful he had ever seen, and he would not be able to tell them apart if someone paid him. Then he said something that made Don Fermino take special notice: He hoped Fermino's horse was as fast as the horse in Las Lomas, since it was the fastest he had ever seen. Many people there thought it was the fastest in all of Mexico.

Fermino got the name of the horse's owner, and for the second time in a couple of weeks he bought a train ticket, this time in the opposite direction from Canitullo, to Las Lomas. He left town the next morning.

Two days later, his foreman Luis received a telegram from Las Lomas, and two days after that, late in the night, after most honest people were in bed, Luis was waiting at the train station for the train from Las Lomas. Together, he and Fermino unloaded a horse from a boxcar, a chestnut, which they then hitched to their wagon and led to Don Fermino's ranch.

Don Fermino had "borrowed" the chestnut from Las Lomas in exchange for one hundred pesos. When Don Fermino had expressed his fear of losing his horse in the coming race, the Las Lomas man understood and agreed to help Fermino with his scheme.

Just before the race was to begin, Luis took El Guapo and galloped him outside of town until the horse was blowing hard and sweated up. As the race started, Luis left El Guapo with another of Fermino's ranch hands behind the livery stable, and then he went and mingled with the crowd watching the race. When the race ended, the rider rode behind the livery stable, jumped off the Las Lomas horse and onto Don Fermino's horse, and then rode onto Main Street. The borrowed chestnut was ridden off unseen by Don Fermino's man behind the livery stable.

But now, Don Fermino, drunk, garrulous, and so ashamed of what he had done, was almost in tears as he told the story. He had always been a man of truth and honor when it came to betting, he claimed, and had never cheated on a bet or refused to pay when he lost. But, he said, he just could not face the prospect of losing El Guapo, the horse he loved so much. And now he had traded away his honor because of that horse, and he was having a hard time accepting it. He said he was even thinking of offering to return the bay to its owner, but he didn't know how he could justify such an act to the bay's owner or to the townspeople without revealing his trickery. And besides, the bay was so beautiful that the thought of giving it back was as painful as the thought of losing his chestnut.

"I may be a *cabrón* and a *jodido,* but look here, *muchacho,* I have the two fastest, loveliest horses in the whole area! Can anything be finer than that?" In spite of his ruined honor, Don Fermino smiled with pride.

I felt forced to agree with him. Nothing could be better than that. Except perhaps owning the chestnut with the white spot on its foreleg.

Mexican Horses
Part II

I was sitting in the backyard just fooling around when I heard Teresa shouting in front. I ran around the house to see what was happening. A cow had wandered into our front yard and was trying to get into the garden to browse. Teresa was shouting at it, waving her arms, while the cow stood undecidedly between fear of the little human and desire to munch on our corn. Olga and Mother came running out the front door, and the cow backed off, lowing as Mother flapped her apron in its face. Father came around the corner to see what the commotion was about.

"That's Filoberto's milk cow," he said. "I'd better take her back."

Filoberto had a large ranch next to our small piece of land and lived about a mile up the road. Father saddled his horse and then looped a rope around the cow's neck. He got on the horse and reached his hand down to me. "Get on," he said. I got on behind him and he handed me the rope. "Hold on to this."

We rode down the road with the cow following behind. As we approached Filoberto's house, the cow suddenly lurched forward and jerked the rope out of my hand. She headed toward the gate at a clumsy gallop, mooing loudly. Benito, Filoberto's son, came off the front porch and grabbed the rope around her neck. We could see Filoberto in one of the corrals off to the side of the house. He saw us, waved, and came toward us.

"*Ay compadre,*" he said to Father. "You have come at a bad time."

"*¿Qué pasa, hombre?*" replied my father. "You look troubled."

"My horse is very sick. He is suffering greatly and I have not been able to make him better. I was getting ready to shoot him when you rode up."

"Your roan?" asked Father. "Charro, your big roan?"

"Yes, Charro. He is like my child. I have waited as long as I can, but now I can wait no more and must put him out of his misery."

We had been riding toward the corral while they talked, and as we dismounted I could see the horse lying still on the ground. Father walked over and knelt beside it. He stroked it, talking to it in a low voice while his fingers ran over the horse's head. He leaned down and smelled the horse's breath.

Father stood up. "He is so beautiful. Are you sure he cannot be cured?"

"I am certain. We have tried everything for three days, but he won't eat and gets weaker and weaker. I just want to end his suffering."

"So you're going to shoot it?"

Filoberto had tears in his voice. "Yes."

"*Compadre,* will you let me take the horse and try to heal it? You're going to shoot him, and you will no longer have him, so why not let me take him? If I cure him I will keep him, but I promise you I will not let him suffer too much if I don't succeed."

"I don't think you can do anything for him, but if you want to try, go ahead."

"If I heal him, will he be mine?"

"Yes. If you give him back his life, he will be yours."

"Then I'll go home and come back with a wagon."

As we got back on the horse, Benito came and gave me the rope we had used to tie around the cow's neck. We left, promising to come right back for the horse.

"Do you really think you can heal the horse?" I asked. The possibility that Charro might be ours excited me greatly.

"I don't know for sure, but there is a chance. When I was a young man, I worked on a ranch with an old *vaquero* who knew more about horses than anyone I've ever met. He taught me things that most people don't know, even those who think of themselves as experts."

"He is so lovely. I hope he will be ours."

"*Si.* One can tell at a glance that this horse is special. My compadre Filoberto is in a hard spot. He wants to end the horse's suffering, but he doesn't want to shoot him; he hopes I can heal the horse, but he also knows that if I do, he will lose the horse anyway. I guess he would rather have the horse alive with someone else than have him dead."

We were now turning off the main road into our front yard. We dismounted and I went to look for Antonio and Roberto while Father hitched the team of mules to the wagon. The four of us then headed back to Filoberto's ranch.

With Filoberto and Benito helping, we managed to get the sick horse on a pallet, then drag it up a ramp onto the back of the wagon. We went back home with Charro too sick and tired to raise his head.

As soon as we got back home, Father had Roberto and me go out and gather a wild shrub Mexicans call *hediondilla*. We came back with our arms loaded. Meanwhile Father had started a fire under a kettle. He stripped the leaves off the shrub and dropped them in the kettle to steep in the boiling water. After a few minutes he ladled out a pot of the mixture, then dipped a blanket into the kettle. He brought out the steaming blanket and draped it over the corral to cool. Finally, when the blanket had cooled sufficiently, he draped it over the horse's torso and had me hold up the horse's head while he forced some of the liquid down its throat.

After that he rolled back part of the blanket and began to massage Charro slowly and gently, talking to him softly all the while. Then he told Antonio, Roberto, and me to help him roll the horse over onto his other side. Father once again soaked the blanket in the liquid and let it cool, then repeated the massage process. After he was done, we left the horse lying there outside the corral.

The next morning Roberto and I had to go gather some more hediondilla, and the whole process was repeated. Toward sundown, we went through it again. The following morning, however, when I went outside I saw Father sitting on the ground by the horse. Charro had managed to lift his head, and Father was stroking it softly, talking to him lovingly. Once more we repeated the massage process. That afternoon Charro stood up and managed to eat a little. My dad was smiling. "I think he's going to be all right," he said.

Within ten days Charro was back to normal. Filoberto could not believe it. "You are a magician," he said to Father. "I swear I was certain that horse would be dead long before now." He hugged Charro's head, and then said, "Well, I gave you my word, and he's yours now. You deserve him."

Of course, that horse became my dad's special friend. Father was almost as careful and loving with him as he was with his family. Sometimes, when the horse was loose, he would follow Father around almost like a dog follows his master.

And then trouble came for Father and his beloved horse. A band of so-called revolutionaries rode into town to steal whatever they could. As always, their cloud of dust gave us advance warning. Immediately people in the village were running around hiding anything of value, no matter how small. As we always had during previous raids, Roberto and I went to get Charro to hide him in the kitchen, knowing that the bandits would not think of going into houses looking for what they prized most after money—horses. They had little hope of ever getting any money from villages like ours, but with luck they might stumble on a horse or two.

We ran into Father, who already had Charro and was walking him toward the house. Then Pamfilo Ortiz, one of the townspeople, called to him. "*¡Compadre!* Don't put your horse in the house. If they look in your house they are sure to find him. I have a special place in the hills where I keep my horse. They'll never find him there!"

I don't know why, but Father handed the reins to Pamfilo, who took the two horses off into the hills. A few minutes later the bandits arrived and spread out through the town, riding up and down streets, shouting at people to come out of their houses.

There was one horse in town that nobody claimed, a beat-up, sway-backed nag that ate whatever anyone fed it. It was barely strong enough to carry the smaller kids in town. When this horse saw the bandits riding in, it spooked and ran out the other end of town toward the foothills. Several members of the gang saw it and galloped after it. Of course, this nag led them directly to where Pamfilo had taken his horse and Father's. They rode back into town leading the two horses by a rope. They had not, of course, bothered with the old nag. The leader of the band took one look at Charro and claimed him as his own.

As a crowd of townspeople gathered, he dismounted his horse, put his saddle on Charro, and got on. The horse began to buck, trying desperately to dump the rider, but the bandit was an excellent horseman and would not be thrown off. Finally the roan gave up and stood exhausted in the middle of the street, panting hoarsely with sweat running off him, soaking the ground.

My father had been watching in the crowd silently, but I could tell what a struggle it was for him to see this stranger not only sitting on his horse, but actually taking it as his own. It was more than he could handle, and he stepped out of the crowd and faced the horseman. "That horse is mine," he said.

The bandit seemed surprised that anyone would question his right to the horse. He looked down on my father from his seat on the horse. Then he spoke: "The Revolution needs horses. Would you deny this horse to the Cause?"

The crowd was dead silent. I was aware that Father's life was in danger if he pressed the matter further, but I also knew that he would not stand quietly by while his beloved Charro was taken from him. Suddenly my mother came running up and placed herself between the bandit and her husband. She was standing there with her back to me, her hair pulled into a bun at the nape, with strands of hair that had loosened in her run to the scene catching the sunlight like a glowing halo. She was there to protect her man, and I think she said the first thing she thought of, since it didn't make much sense.

"Take the horse," she said, "and when you get another one, you can send this one back to us."

I guess the bandit wanted to avoid a shooting if he could because he immediately responded to Mother's statement. "Yes, I'll do that. I'll get another horse at the next village and then I'll send this one back to you."

Father knew this was nonsense, but when he tried to speak again, Mother whirled around to face him. "Let's go home," she said.

"Wait a minute!" Father started again. "I want . . ."

"Let's go home!" said Mother again, and for the only time in my life I saw her put a hand on him in anger. She grabbed his arm and started forcefully leading him through the crowd. Father turned his head and tried again to say something to the man who was stealing his horse, but my mom only pulled him away harder, whispering fiercely, "Shut up and go home!" I don't know which was more shocking to me, seeing my dad lose Charro or hearing my mom talk to Father that way.

So the man kept the horse and my dad kept his life, although I don't think Father ever recovered from losing Charro. He was dispirited for days afterward, and several months later, when we had lost all our savings because of the Revolution and he and Mother decided to leave Mexico and emigrate to the United States, I know the loss of his horse was one of the main reasons he decided to leave his homeland. How could he stay when the friend whose life he had saved, his special, beloved friend, had been ripped away from him forever?

🐕 Coyote

My friend Enrique often went on walks alone into the low, rolling hills on the outskirts of San Cristobal. He would leave early in the morning with a water bottle and some corn tortillas and usually not return until nightfall. I wondered about Enrique's trips into the hills, and I often wished he would ask me to go with him, or at least tell me what he did there. But as far as I knew, he never took anyone with him, and he never talked to me or anyone else about what he saw or did.

Enrique lived with his father and Chencho, a brother my age, about a half-mile from town, toward the river. His father worked for the railroad and was often gone for days at a time. Enrique's mother had died a few days after Chencho was born, from childbed fever. So Enrique was pretty much a thirteen-year-old who took care of himself and his brother. I was his closest friend, but he never seemed to need anyone else as the rest of us did.

One morning Enrique showed up at my house and asked if I wanted to go for a walk with him up into the hills. In amazement, I quickly answered yes. I told Mother I was going with Enrique and would probably be gone most of the day. Mother thought Enrique was a little strange, but he was always polite and serious around her, so she trusted his judgment more than she trusted mine. She hesitated for a moment, then nodded her assent.

We walked west out of town and onto *la bajada,* the slope that rose to the hills that footed the sierra. We walked up the hills in silence, and just as I was beginning to think that walking was all Enrique did on these trips, he stopped at the top of one of the hills and sat down in the shade of a low mesquite tree. I sat down beside him. From this point we could see all of San Cristobal in the distance below us. By now the sun was high and hot.

"Let's sit here and be quiet," he whispered to me. "Don't move and don't talk."

I nodded, glad to sit and catch my breath. At first, the only sound was my heavy breathing, but before long that too died down. Gradually the desert came alive again. Soon the flies were zooming past and the locusts whirring; a gleaming black beetle continued his purposeful journey across the hot sand; a gray rabbit came hopping slowly by, pausing every few seconds to peer around, his nose twitching; a drab brown bird flew to its nest woven in the hollow of the trunk of a *palo verde,* the desert tree with an intense green trunk; from afar, came the soft, haunting sound of a mourning dove. In the distance, the heat waves made the plants and rocks seem liquid and mysterious. Occasionally, a drop of sweat would slide down my brow and into my eyes, stinging and blurring my vision, but I sat still, squeezing my eyes tight from time to time, but making no move to rub them clear. Everything around us was moving, chirping, buzzing.

We sat until I was so uncomfortable that I was sure I would have to do something—scratch, sneeze, stretch.

Then I saw a movement in a saddle formed by two adjacent buttes below us. At first I thought it was the heat waves rippling the sand, but then I saw for sure that something was there, something that just seemed to materialize out of the sand itself. Without moving I glanced sideways at Enrique to see if he too had seen anything. He was glancing at me, his face excited. I shifted my gaze back down to the saddle, and now I could clearly see what was moving—it was a coyote.

The coyote padded across the saddle and stopped in front of what looked like a rock lying in the sand. He reached down with his muzzle and started nudging at the rock until he turned it over, and then he sat on his haunches watching it intently. Coyote sat as still as we were, waiting patiently by the rock. Suddenly something sprouted from the rock, like a short stick jutting out of the solid mass. Coyote moved quickly, a sudden blur as his jaws closed on the stick. He shook his head and the stick broke off in his mouth. He ate it, and then he sat again, unmoving. A short while later another stick jerked out, and once again Coyote moved, snapping it off, and chewing it. By now, I was thoroughly confused, and glanced again at Enrique, whose eyes were still focused on the scene below.

The process was repeated two more times, and then Coyote trotted off, disappearing into the desert sand as quickly as he had appeared.

"Let's go look," said Enrique as he stood up and started down toward the saddle. I hurried after him.

The "rock" was a desert turtle. "Coyote turns the turtle over on its back," explained Enrique. "Soon the sun starts to roast the turtle in its shell, so he sticks a leg out to try to get rid of some of the heat. When he does,

Coyote bites the leg off. Four legs and he has a full meal, and Turtle dies in his shell." The dying turtle now had its head stuck out of the shell as it drew its last breaths.

"Come on," said Enrique. "Let me show you another place."

We continued on up toward the base of the sierra, and shortly I could see a splotch of green that we were headed toward. It was a small grove of cottonwoods, reeds, and grasses growing at the mouth of an arroyo that snaked down from the sierra and drained at the top of the bajada. There was a small rivulet of water running off the mountain and collecting into a natural pond about four feet deep at its deepest and ten feet across. Enrique took off his clothes and stepped into the water. I followed.

The cold water was a shock at first, but in a few moments I felt refreshed and invigorated as we splashed around.

"Did you know that Coyote is the smartest animal in the world?" asked Enrique. "He can disappear and reappear whenever he wants. You think you've got him, and he's gone. You see a shadow under a tree, look away for a second, look back, and the shadow's gone. It wasn't a shadow; it was Coyote. He can sit and wait, much, much longer than I can. Sometimes at night you can hear him laughing at everyone that thinks they can outsmart him, and sometimes in the moonlight he sings about how lonely he is. He knows more about surviving than any other creature, including humans." He paused, then added quietly, "Coyote is who I try to be like."

He lay on his back for a while, looking up at the sky. Then he stood up, stepped out of the water, and lay in the sun to dry. I lay beside him, thinking of Coyote.

"Coyote uses this pond too, and not just to drink or cool off. I've seen him step into the pond until the water is up to his belly. Then he stands and waits and waits. Eventually, the fleas that are on his legs move up until they are above the water line on his back and sides and tail. After a long time, he steps into deeper water until only his head is sticking above the water. Then he waits more, patiently, patiently. Again the fleas move up until his whole head is covered with them. Then Coyote ducks his head underwater, shakes it, and then pulls it out of the water. He does this several times until most of the fleas have been carried off by the water. I've seen him do this more than once."

We sat in the shade beside the pond and ate some tortillas and beef jerky that Enrique had brought. It was quiet and peaceful.

"Chencho tells me your family might be leaving Mexico to go north, al Norte, *a los Estados Unidos*," asked Enrique. "Is that true?"

"I don't know for sure, but I think it's going to happen. A bank in Nogales stole all the money Father had saved up, and my mom's been worried sick because of the revolutionaries stealing and taking everything, and killing innocent people. She's afraid Father might get hurt or the revolutionaries might take Antonio or Berto away. Anyway, they say there's a good chance we'll leave Mexico. That means I would be an *Americano*." The idea of my being an American seemed so ludicrous that I started to giggle. "Can you imagine that? Me, an *Americano!*"

Enrique laughed. "You'll have to become a *huero*—dye your hair blond, wear a ten-gallon hat like the *Tejanos,* and trade your huaraches for cowboy boots.

Then you can call everybody 'Pahdner' and 'Metsicans'."

We both laughed uncontrollably at the image.

"I don't really want to go," I said, "but I think it's going to happen."

Enrique sat up. "Let me tell you a story about Coyote that Fidelio told me a couple of years ago. When God created all the animals that live in the desert, He told them to live together in peace, and then He left them to behave as they would. All the animals had legs and lived on the land. None could fly, or swim, or run fast. They all got along well, except Coyote. He was always hanging around watching the other animals and playing jokes on them. He would tell Rabbit that Snake was hiding in the arroyo to ambush him, and then tell Snake that Rabbit and Eagle had set a trap to catch him under the mesquite. Soon nobody trusted anybody else, and everybody was arguing with everybody else.

"'Who told you I was going to ambush you?' Snake asked Rabbit.

"'Yes,' added Eagle, 'and where did you hear that Rabbit and I were plotting against you?'

"The answer to all these questions was always, 'Coyote.'

"So the animals went to God and told him that Coyote was causing all kinds of trouble with his jokes, and nobody trusted anybody anymore and there was no more peace in the desert. 'Give us some way to get away from this troublemaker!'

"'Find coyote and bring him here,' said God. 'I will take care of this problem.'

"But Coyote was hiding in the chaparral, and he heard everything the animals and God said, so he decided to lie low for a while, until things cooled down. He found a burrow in the hills and he lay there quietly while the other animals ran all around the desert calling his name.

"When they couldn't find him, the animals went back to God and told him. So God said, 'Very well, then. I will not punish Coyote. Instead I will give each creature gifts that he can use to get away from Coyote when he wants. Line up, and I will award you each with your gifts.' Eagle went first and was given the gift of high flight and sharp eyes; Fish was given the ability to swim and breathe under water; Snake could crawl and hide in small holes; Rabbit could run fast and dodge; Cactus Wren could fly and dart quickly, and so on.

"When all the animals had gotten their gifts, God said, 'Now, where is Coyote? If Coyote were here, I could give him special gifts too.'

"Again, Coyote had hidden in the bushes, watching and listening. 'Oh no,' thought Coyote. 'You don't fool me that easily. If I step forward you'll only punish me for causing trouble. I'll just keep quiet.'

"And ever since then, all the other animals use their special gift to keep away from Coyote." Enrique paused for a moment, with a storyteller's talent for emphasizing the main point of his tale. "And since then, all the other animals think Coyote outsmarted himself, and was left with no special gift. But Fidelio told me that whether he knew it or not, God had given Coyote the greatest gifts of all: Coyote trusts no one, not even God. Coyote watches everything in hiding. He sleeps with one eye open. He sees the other animals do dumb things, and he laughs. He's an outsider because he is an artist, an artist of survival. Always study Coyote and his ways, Fidelio told me."

It was mid-afternoon, so we started heading back toward town. We were mostly silent, as I thought about the story of Coyote. When we got to the fork in the road where Enrique went one way to his home and I went the other to town, he stopped.

"I'm sorry that you're leaving," he said.

"Me too. I'm kinda scared about going north. I don't know much about *gringos* or how the *Norteamericanos* live. I wish we would just stay here."

"You'll be all right. Just remember Coyote, and use all of Coyote's gifts."

We shook hands, and he headed toward the river while I walked on toward town.

🦜 Mockingbird

The boy ran down Main Street shouting, "*¡Hay vienen los bandidos!*" The bandits were coming! Suddenly our sleepy little town of San Cristobal was fully awake, people running in all directions. In Mexico in 1917, bands of armed horsemen roamed northern Sonora, calling themselves "revolutionaries." They would occasionally ride into San Cristobal, looking for guns, money, and horses. My brother Roberto and I went running home to put Father's horse in the kitchen to hide him from these bandits. They never thought to look in our house for a horse. Once we had the horse in the kitchen, Mother sent us off to look for Father. Roberto ran one way and I another. I found my father in the cantina/pool hall that he owned and ran.

"I know, I know," he said to me. "Just stay calm and nothing will happen."

I heard a group of horses galloping down the street and then gunshots. Through the window I could see about a dozen armed horsemen shouting and firing their guns and rifles into the air. They stopped in the center of town and dismounted, demanding to see the head of the community.

As the village comisario, my father was obligated to face the men. When he stepped out into the street, the leader pulled a pistol on him and demanded any money the village had on hand. He explained to them that San Cristobal was a very poor ranching community with no money or food to spare. Then he took them to his office across the street and opened the village safe. Inside were some official papers and a rusty old revolver that no longer fired. I was peeping into the office through a window as the jefe of the group put his gun against my father's head and threatened to shoot if he did not produce money and horses. Father explained calmly again that there was neither in the village, which had been drained dry by other revolutionaries so that now there was not enough for the villagers themselves. For a few moments the leader stood with the gun pressed against Father's temple. Finally he muttered, "*¡Vámonos!*" They scattered the papers around the office, took the broken revolver, and left.

Suddenly my mother came running down the street and grabbed me tightly, shouting for my father. He came out of the office and we stood in the street hugging each other, my mother and I crying.

Sometimes we would be awakened in the middle of the night by armed men on horseback, frightening, short-tempered men on the run, seeking money or beef. Although only nine, I was fully aware of the danger we were living in. My poor mother, trying so hard to keep her eight children safe, would behave as normally as possible, but I could tell how frightened and nervous she really was.

Before the Revolution began in 1910, her married life had been hard but happy. The beautiful seventeen-year-old that Father had married turned out to have a core of steel. She ran the household, organized chores, and saw that work was distributed evenly among her eight kids, according to our abilities. My father consulted her on matters many Mexican men would never think of consulting their wives on. He wouldn't think of buying a horse or cow without her agreement, and once he wanted to buy a small plot of land from a neighbor, but she felt it unnecessary, so he turned the offer down.

But eventually the danger and stress of the Revolution drained her so that it took all her will to keep some normalcy in her family's life. One day there was a battle being fought some miles from San Cristobal, but close enough that we could hear the artillery shells exploding in the distance. All that day the adults were quiet and serious, wondering if the battle would move in our direction. That evening at dinner, with the noise of battle still audible, as my mother stood up to get something, she fainted and fell to the floor. Father picked her up hurriedly and carried her into their bedroom, gently placing her on the bed. We younger kids stood around, too scared to cry, while the older children helped father revive her. There were no doctors in San Cristobal, just a couple of *curanderas*, herbal healers, one of whom came quickly and prepared an herbal concoction for her.

The battle was over the next day, but my mother remained in bed for several days afterward. When she did get out of bed, she was pale and weak. I was shocked at how frail my mother suddenly appeared. But it was not too long before she once again willed control of the household and her children.

One day my father came home with a young mockingbird he had found fallen out of its nest, too young to fly. He gave it to Mother, who took it gently in her hand and quickly had us digging outside for worms and grubs to feed it. Mother cared for the bird as she would her own child. She named it Horacio, and got a cage to put it in, although most of the time it wandered freely about the house. In a few weeks it was flying, but never very far from the house or Mother. For the bird, my mother was his mother too.

In the mornings she would uncover the cage Horacio slept in, and the bird would begin singing. We all knew he was singing especially for her. He would balance on the edge of her hand while she brought him up to her mouth, and he would take bits of chewed-up tortilla from between her lips. Then he would fly outside and flutter around the garden while Mother irrigated or weeded. He would land on her shoulder, and she would talk to him while he chirped back at her cheerfully. At night she would hold him up to her mouth again, and even though there was no food for him, he would carefully place his beak between her lips. This ritual before his going into the cage to sleep was a delight for us kids. We would joke that he was kissing her goodnight before going to bed.

One day Father left San Cristobal to go to Nogales, on the U.S. border, where he had deposited more than two thousand pesos he and Mother had saved over several years. To get to Nogales required a half-day's journey on horseback to Santa Ana, and then a half-day's train ride from there. He had left his money in Nogales because other, closer banks were subject to hold-ups by the "revolutionaries." Now he wanted to withdraw the money to buy some cattle. He was gone for three days.

When he returned he barely responded to the shouts and hugs of his children. He and Mother went into their bedroom to talk. In a few moments we could hear Mother's voice rising and then some half-strangled sobs. Shortly after, Father emerged grim and tight-lipped. We found out later that when he went to withdraw his money, the bank paid him in pesos printed by Pancho Villa, utterly worthless, which the bank had been forced to take at gunpoint by Villa's troops in exchange for regular currency. When my father complained that he had given the bank good money and the bank had returned worthless paper, the bank manager responded that Father only had two thousand pesos of worthless paper; the bank had millions.

My mother began having more fainting spells after this, and in fear for her health, Father decided he had had enough of the revolutionary anarchy. He and Mother discussed the situation over several days and then made the difficult decision to take the family, leave our homeland, and emigrate to the United States.

Father wrote to his uncle in Douglas, Arizona, explaining his decision to go to the United States and requesting any help he could give us in setting up in a new country. The uncle wrote back urging us to come quickly. He owned a ranch outside of Douglas and had recently bought an adjacent piece of land with a ranch house on it. If we came to Arizona, we could live in this house and develop the ranch, which had been abandoned and was in disrepair.

The next few days after receiving his uncle's letter are a blur of hectic activity in my memory. My father sold everything we owned for whatever he could get—house, furniture, and livestock—with the exception of a team of mules to pull a wagon and his personal horse. We would take only clothes, a few personal belongings, a little money, and ourselves to our new country. And, of course, Horacio the mockingbird.

We loaded the wagon with a few steamer trunks and boxes and eight kids to begin the six-hour trip to Santa Ana, where Father would sell the remaining livestock and we would board the train to Douglas. We said tearful goodbyes to our friends and set out early in the morning. Antonio, my oldest brother, drove the team of mules while the other kids crowded into the wagon or took turns riding behind Father on his horse. Mother sat on the front seat next to Antonio, with Horacio in his cage on her lap. At first she kept the cage uncovered, but poor Horacio seemed so distressed by the commotion that she covered the cage with her shawl and placed it under the seat, hoping the bird would sleep through most of the journey.

It was early July and the hot trip through the Sonora desert seemed endless. I remember sitting in the back of a bouncing wagon, being jarred until my butt was so tender I would jump off the wagon and walk beside it. Then the heat would start to make me dizzy, and I would clamber aboard the wagon again. The only pleasant part of the trip was riding horseback, sitting behind my father for half an hour or so, until it was another child's turn. About midday we came into Santa Ana.

We rode first to the train station to buy ten tickets to Douglas. Everyone began unloading the wagon so that Father could take it to the livery stable to sell along with the mules and his horse. As boxes and trunks were being unloaded at the station, Mother reached under the seat and brought out Horacio in his cage. She uncovered it to see the bird lying at the bottom of the cage. She called to him, but the bird did not move. She reached in and took the bird gently, but it was now obvious: Horacio was dead.

In all of my nine years I had never felt such a shock as I did at that instant. I didn't know why, but I was so frightened I started crying. Mother dropped the bird wordlessly on the loading dock of the station.

My brother Roberto picked it up and said, "We have to bury him."

Mother turned on him savagely. "Don't be stupid! We don't have time to be burying anyone! Take it and throw it away, quick! It's just a stupid bird!"

Roberto started crying. "Mama! It's Horacio! We have to bury . . ."

"THROW IT AWAY!"

Antonio took the bird from Roberto and walked off with it. He was back a minute later and continued unloading the wagon silently. Father walked shyly to Mother and tried to put his arm around her, but she pushed him away. "You should be helping unload the wagon," she said to him. "Olga! Maria Elena! Don't just stand there like fools. Get this stuff off the wagon." She grabbed a box and slammed it down on the loading dock.

The train ride to Douglas took five hours. During the entire ride Mother sat at a window looking out, not speaking to anyone, even ignoring her wild brood as we ran up and down the aisles of the railroad cars. This in itself was frightening. Not once did she rein us in or express concern that we were behaving like savages instead of respectable people. She just sat and looked out the window, grim and dry-eyed.

I don't recall much about the border crossing, so I guess there were no difficulties in acquiring a new homeland. I do remember my uncle meeting us at Customs. He was large and hearty. He had not seen my father since my parents' wedding eighteen years earlier. He grabbed

Father's hand and shook it vigorously and embraced my mom, who uttered a few polite phrases and then stepped back. We loaded up in his wagon and rode to his ranch a few miles outside of Douglas.

Two or three days later we were taken to the ranch that would be our home. It had been abandoned for several years, and all the windows were broken out and the doors removed. There were swallow nests and droppings in every room. The kitchen had been papered with newspapers, some of which were hanging down in strips. I remember looking closely at the newspapers and being shocked that I could not read one word of them.

"They're in English," said Antonio, "That's why you can't read them."

"It's not too bad," said Father. "We can fix it up in no time, and then we'll have a real nice home. Look here, woman, we can get a good stove, and I'll put in a solid table, a round one, one that we can all sit at and eat. It won't take long at all."

Mother just stood with her arms crossed, looking out the glassless window at the weed-choked yard. She looked different, tired and worn. She did not respond to Father's casting about for enthusiasm.

We spent the first night sleeping outside on the ground, and early the next morning the clean-up began in earnest, although Mother slept late, and it was Father who doled out the chores to the kids. Weeds were chopped and piled, the floors swept, walls stripped and washed, while Father and Antonio went into Douglas to get food, pots, pans, and dishes. Roberto and I wanted to go too, but we had to stay and help with the cleaning. But I was a little scared of going anyway. There would be all those *gringos* speaking a language I knew nothing about.

The cleaning continued for the next few days, but the house just didn't feel like a home. Mother was still not involved with the chores or running the family. She did everything like a machine, with little care and no enthusiasm. It was bad enough that she no longer smiled or laughed, but that she didn't give orders or scold us kids was truly disturbing.

After several days Father approached Roberto and me and told us to go into the countryside and check bird nests to see if we could find a mockingbird. We were to catch it and bring it directly to him, and we were not to mention it to Mother.

Roberto and I set out, spotting nests and shinnying up trees to see what was in them. Every nest we looked in was empty. Finally, we noticed a nest high up a palo verde tree, and since it was my turn, I climbed up the tree until my head was level with the nest. I stretched my neck and looked in. Peering back at me were two yellow eyes set in a wedge-shaped head. A small rattlesnake had curled up inside the nest, for whatever reason, and it was not pleased at having been disturbed. It set off its rattle and I went tumbling down the tree, smacking into several branches on my way down. By the time I hit the ground I had cuts and scratches on my face and arms, and the front of my shirt had been ripped almost in two.

Roberto and I decided not to do any more searching that day, and we went back to report to Father. When we got home my shirt was bloody from my cuts and one of my eyes was swelling shut. We were outside the front door explaining to Father what had happened when Mother stepped outside. She saw me and stopped short.

"What on earth happened to you?" She turned to Father. "What mischief have you had these children getting into?"

She was upset, but I was happy to have her notice me for the first time since we left Santa Ana.

"How did you ruin your clothes?" she said angrily. She grabbed Roberto by the shoulders and shook him roughly. "What have you two been doing?" she shouted in his face.

Roberto started to cry. "Father wanted us to get a mockingbird for you! We were looking for one when Rafael saw a snake instead and he fell out of the tree."

"A mockingbird!?" She faced Father. "A mockingbird!"

He looked down sheepishly and mumbled, "I only wanted to help make you feel better again."

She turned and hurried into the house. We stood outside for a few moments, and then Father walked in after her. Roberto and I followed. She was slumped at our new table, the upper half of her body sprawled on the tabletop. She was not just crying: there was a wail of such anguish and pain that it made me reel back in terror. Some of the girls heard the sound and rushed into the kitchen. There we all stood around the table while Mother's cries rose to heaven. Father motioned us to leave, and we all stepped back outside where Roberto and I tried to explain in hushed tones what had happened.

When Father called us back in, Mother was in their room in bed. He heated up some beans while Maria Elena made tortillas, and then we ate in silence.

That night Roberto and I lay in bed whispering, wondering what would become of us now that Mother was acting so strange. "I hate this country," said Roberto. "Everything has gone bad ever since we left San Cristobal.

Maybe we can talk Father into taking us all back." When I realized Roberto was sobbing softly, I joined in.

The next morning I awoke to sounds in the kitchen. Roberto was up and getting dressed. Still upset, I dressed and followed him into the kitchen. Mother was at the table mixing up a big bowl of masa for tortillas. "Maria Elena," she shouted. "Go see if the chickens laid any eggs. Olga, you go pull some grass for the rabbits. Teresa, get some water for the rabbits and the chickens." She turned and saw me standing there. "What are you looking at? Don't you know your father needs some help outside? Are you waiting for an invitation?"

"No, Mama."

"Roberto! Go get some firewood! How am I supposed to cook without firewood?" Then, looking at me again, "Are you still standing here? I told you your father needs help! Just how do you think we're going to survive in a new country if we don't all work? Don't you want to help?"

"*Si*, Mama! *¡Si!*"

I hurried outside to my father, who was chopping weeds, clearing the irrigation ditch that would water our newly dug garden. He looked up at me and then turned back to the ditch. I stood there without speaking for a minute.

"Papa?"

He stopped and turned to me again.

"What has happened, Papa? What is going on?"

He gave me a quick smile. "Everything is all right, son. We're going to be just fine. Here," he said, handing me his hoe. "Get to work."

"Yessir," I said, "Yessir." And I started chopping with a will.

Carnival

We had been in our new country for about two weeks, with my dad just starting to work for his uncle Oscar when he gave him a few dollars and told him to take some of the kids to a carnival that was set up on the outskirts of Douglas. There was not enough money for Father to take everyone, so we drew straws to see who would go. Antonio, Maria Elena, and I were the winners. We left that evening at sundown, walking the two miles to the carnival.

The carnival was the most amazing thing I had ever seen in my life. It was dreamland. There were bright lights strung everywhere, loud music blaring from all around, barkers shouting, a gigantic Ferris wheel, all sorts of rides and games, and big canvas posters with paintings of wild animals, freaks, and beautiful young ladies. People of all ages were crowded in the midway, some strolling, some shouting and laughing at the gambling booths, others trying their luck at different games. Most of the shouting and talking was in English, incomprehensible to me, but every now and then I would hear a bit of Spanish, and I would look around to see if I could spot other Mexicans in the crowd, wondering if this was as exciting to them as it was to me. I held Father's hand tightly, almost fainting from all the stimulation. *This is truly like a dream,* I thought. *Nothing in Mexico was ever like this.*

Father gave a dollar to Antonio and Maria Elena and told them to stick together and that he would stay with me. We would meet in an hour by the Ferris wheel. We wandered from booth to booth, watching, and occasionally playing a game. I tried popping balloons with darts and throwing coins into a glass, but I won nothing. Father threw three balls into a basket and won a glass pitcher, which he gave to me to hold and care for. I took my responsibility very seriously, holding it tightly and never setting it down, even when we rode on the Ferris wheel. I was proud of my dad; even in a foreign country he could play a game and win. At one booth there was music coming from inside a tent with a picture of a woman with her skirt hiked up so that one stockinged leg was showing. I asked Father what game was in there, and he just laughed and said it was not for us.

We met Antonio and Maria Elena after our ride on the Ferris wheel, and we began the walk back to Uncle's house. Maria Elena was carrying a small doll that Antonio had won in one of the games. We were too excited to do much talking as we walked in the dark. I was still overwhelmed by the fairy world of the carnival. What other magic treasures did our new homeland hold?

At first we walked along the road in the darkness. Behind us we could hear the music growing dimmer and dimmer, and soon we could barely see the glow of the lights. Then my dad led us off the road and started walking across a farm field. "This is a short cut to Uncle Oscar's house," he said. "I've come this way several times with him."

We stumbled on across the furrowed field in complete darkness for what seemed like hours to me. Now I was tired and sleepy, but I still refused to let anyone else carry the pitcher Father had won. I guess I was pretty much sleepwalking, and once, when Father stopped to try to get his bearings, I walked right into him and fell. He picked me up. "I'm afraid we're lost," he said. "I thought sure we were going the right way, but we've come too far. We should have hit the road to Uncle's by now."

We stood in the field for a while, looking in all directions for some sort of landmark or guide, but in the darkness we could see nothing. We weren't even sure we could find our way back to the road we had left so long ago. And then Antonio said, "I think I see a light!" He pointed. We all looked but I could see nothing.

"You're right," said Father. "Over there." We started walking again. Again I was sleepwalking, stumbling every few minutes. The light was at a farmhouse, and as we approached there was a wild commotion of barking dogs. That woke me up for a moment and I held tightly to Father's leg. Fortunately the dogs were inside a fenced yard. We stood at the gate, and in a moment the front door opened and a man stood on the porch looking into the darkness.

The man shouted something in English at us in the dark.

"We're lost," shouted my father in Spanish. "We need some directions."

The man shouted something again.

"We're lost," repeated Father in Spanish, louder this time. Then, "No espeeke Ingliss."

A woman's voice came from inside the house, asking the man a question.

He answered her, and in a moment she was at the door with a lantern and a rifle, which she gave to the man. He stepped off the porch with the lantern in one hand and the rifle pointed at us in the other. She said something in a voice of concern. He shouted at the dogs, kicking at them, and they quieted down and backed off. He came within a few feet of the gate and held the lantern up. He seemed to relax a little when he saw that we were obviously a family. He asked something again, and again my dad told him we were lost.

The man struggled to come up with what Spanish he knew. "*¿No camino?*" he asked.

"*Si, si. No tenemos camino,*" answered Father. "*Estamos perdidos.*"

In the light of the lantern we could see the man shrug. "*¿Dónde?*" he asked.

"*Oscar Romero. Buscamos a Oscar Romero.*"

"Oscar!" said the man in relief. "*Mira,*" he said, pointing back toward the direction from which we had just come. "Oscar Romero. *Poquito.* Oscar."

Father thanked him and we set off once again. I lost all track of time as we stumbled on across the fields, but eventually we got to the road. Now the walking was easier, and just knowing that Uncle Oscar's was not far away made it more bearable for me.

And then it struck me. I no longer had the pitcher Father had won at the carnival! I must have left it lying on the ground one of the times I had stumbled in the dark.

First I thought of turning around and going to look for it, but I quickly realized I would never find it in the dark. Next I thought that if I didn't mention it, maybe Father would forget about the prize he had won. I knew that would never happen, so I took the third option. I started crying. My dad knelt down and hugged me. "We're almost there," he said.

"I lost it! I lost your pitcher!" I bawled.

"That's all right," he said, "it's all right. I don't care about the pitcher. Let's just go home."

But it wasn't all right. He had won it by showing his skill in a foreign country, our new country, and I had ruined it. It was as if he had won nothing at all.

When we finally got to Uncle's house, all the adults were up waiting for us, worried that it was so late. Father laughed and said we were late because we had taken a short cut.

"Well," said Uncle Oscar to me, rumpling my hair, "How did you like the carnival?"

I didn't respond, but just staggered over to the bed I shared with Roberto and fell into a dreamless sleep.

 # Schooling
Part I

hen we emigrated from Mexico to Douglas, Arizona, I was nine years old and spoke no English. I had gone to school in San Cristobal and could read and write Spanish, but English was totally foreign to me. We came to the United States in early spring, but since there was so much work to be done on the ranch we moved into, we didn't start school until the following September. In school I learned what it meant to be Mexican along the U.S./Mexico border; I learned about prejudice and racism.

All of us, including Antonio, who was fifteen years old, were placed into the first grade since we could not speak English. Ernesto, the youngest in the family to start school, was six. Antonio was upset and embarrassed at having to be in class with the little kids, but Father wanted him to learn to read and write English, so Antonio agreed to go to school until he had learned the basics of the language. Olga, at seventeen my oldest sister, had a serious boyfriend in Douglas and did not enter school. She married within a year of our arrival in the United States.

Our first day in school we were herded into the first-grade classroom by Antonio. The first thing I noticed was that all the Mexican kids were sitting in one portion of the classroom while the Anglo kids were sitting in another. I saw one Anglo boy who was about my age; all the other Anglos seemed to be six or seven years old. I think Antonio was relieved to see two or three Mexican kids about his age.

Within minutes of my our entry into the classroom, the teacher, Mrs. Bookstaver, was speaking to us, obviously telling us to do something, but since we spoke no English, we had no idea what she wanted. One of the Mexican kids sitting next to me whispered for me to go to the front of the class. I went forward, followed by my brothers and sisters. When I got to the teacher's desk, she had me lean forward while she put her hands on my head and ran her fingers through my hair. For a confused moment I thought she was caressing me, but her fingers were so strong and harsh. Then I realized she was checking for lice. I could see several of the Anglo kids out of the corner of my eye, smirking as I stood there as humiliated as I had ever been. From that point on, every Monday morning all the Mexican kids had to go up to her desk so she could do her check. I don't recall that she ever caught anyone with lice, but the checks continued anyway.

Spanish was the only language most of us in the Mexican section of the class knew, but since speaking Spanish was strictly forbidden on the school grounds, we did not do much talking, either in the classroom or out. The principal, Mr. Davis, was a retired army major who still wore a military jacket and jodhpurs. He walked around the school grounds with a quirt, which he slapped lightly against the sides of his pantlegs. If he sneaked up on us while we were speaking Spanish, the quirt would swish through the air and slash against our bottoms or the backs of our legs.

"Are you speaking Spanish?" Whap!

"Me no speakeh Spanish!"

"Don't lie to me! I heard you!" Whap!

"Me no speakeh Spanish!"

Whap!

Then the child turned away, muttering, "*Viejo puto, hijo de tu chingada . . .*"

"What did you say? Did I hear you speaking Spanish again?" Whap!

"Me no speakeh Spanish!"

And so it went. Those few Mexican kids who spoke some English would coach the rest of us during recess or the lunch hour. I don't remember the specific process of learning English, but I guess concern for my physical welfare motivated me strongly because I did learn it.

I remember the classroom as a place of terror where none of the Mexicans ever said a word unless they were specifically called upon, something that almost never happened unless the student was being punished. One day, my sister Teresa, then about ten years old, forgot to go pee during the afternoon recess. She kept squirming in her seat but was too frightened to ask for permission to go to the bathroom, which she would have had to do in Spanish anyway since she did not know the proper words in English. I don't recall any Mexican kid ever asking permission to go, so we weren't sure what the teacher would have done if we had. I guess we just assumed something terrible would be done to us, like making us pee in front of the class.

Poor Teresa was twisting and turning in her desk, looking desperately at the clock as it became a contest between time and her bladder control. By now every one of the Mexican kids was aware of her problem, and we suffered along with her. About fifteen minutes before the final bell rang, Teresa lost the struggle. She hid her face in her hands and sobbed as softly as she could while a puddle appeared under her desk. Those of us who were aware of what had happened did not say a word, and when the last bell rang, we all ran out shielding Teresa in the middle of the group.

The next morning the teacher gave a talk to the Mexican section of the class. I didn't understand everything she said, but I had a pretty good idea. She talked about bathrooms and what they were for, and how some us may be used to behaving like animals and peeing anywhere and anytime we wanted, but in America, and especially in her classroom, we would behave like proper human beings and use the facilities provided for the purpose. At home, we could act like beasts and pee on the floor, but if we ever did that in her class, she would make us clean it up while the rest of the class watched and then send us home and not let us return until we had a note saying we had been potty trained.

If we—not only my family, but all the Mexican kids—had not supported each other, I don't see how we could have survived the lessons of school. We stuck together on the playground, partially because we chose to, and partially because we were not particularly welcome with the Anglo kids. We empathized with each other's problems in school, and we often worked to ease these problems as much as we could.

As the first semester drew to a close, toward the end of December, we began to hear talk of a Christmas party to be held in the classroom on the last day of the semester. Gradually the excitement began to grow among the students, including the Mexican kids. There would be decorations, cookies, fruit, candies, and even Christmas gifts for the kids. We began to look forward to the great day, not only because of the party, but also because for a couple of weeks afterward we would be released from the torment of the classroom.

After lunch on the last day, the parents of the Anglo kids began to show up with packages, bags of goodies, and decorations for the classroom. Mrs. Bookstaver walked to the rear of the room where the Mexican kids sat and had us all stand up. She then led us out of the classroom and into the playground. There were Mexican kids from other classes sitting at some tables in the playground. Mrs. Bookstaver took us to the same tables and told us to stay there until she called for us. She turned and headed back toward the classroom.

It was cold and we huddled together trying to figure out what was going on while we waited to join the class party.

One of the older kids laughed. "What do you mean you don't know what's happening? What *pendejos!* This is our Christmas party!" He hooted loudly. "Have some cookies! Do you want some candy? Let me help you open your presents!" He laughed again, but it sounded hollow.

We didn't want to believe him, but as we sat in the cold, the truth of what he said became inescapable. A few kids tried to start a game of tag, but it died almost as soon as it started. Mostly, we sat and shivered, and tried to pretend that we didn't give a damn about their party. Then the final bell rang and Mrs. Bookstaver came out and told us to go home.

We started for home, and one of the kids turned to me and said, "Merry Christmas!"

I started to respond with *Feliz Navidad,* but changed my mind. "Yeah. Merry Christmas."

# Schooling
Part II

"Hey Meskin!"

Someone grabbed me from behind and pushed me so hard that I fell forward on the playground.

"I don't like Meskins!"

I rolled over and saw a freckled, redheaded kid standing over me. I didn't know him, but he seemed to be very angry at me. I stood up.

"I said I don't like Meskins!" he shouted in my face. "What are you going to do about that?"

I glanced quickly at the kids who had gathered around us. Where was my big brother Roberto? The redhead pushed me again, and I stumbled backward against one of the kids encircling us. He kept me from falling, but he then jumped back in exaggerated horror.

"Ugh! The dirty Meskin touched me! Oh no, now I gotta go wash!"

"You better take a bath," someone added.

The redhead was coming at me again with hate in his eyes. I bolted and ran, leaving the group behind laughing and jeering. "I'll get you, Meskin!" shouted the redhead.

I spent the rest of the lunch period huddled behind a hedge that ran along the wall of my classroom. I didn't know the redheaded kid, but I had been in school long enough to know why he hated me. I didn't understand it, but I knew that my being Mexican was enough to make other kids and some teachers hate me. I couldn't see a way to fight against that, so I just stayed hiding behind the hedge until the bell rang.

At the end of the school day I made sure to stay close to Roberto as we left the classroom in case I should run into the redhead. Sure enough, he was waiting for me on the playground.

"Hey!" he shouted and started coming toward us.

I grabbed Roberto's arm. "Let's go this way," I said, hurrying away from my tormentor.

He ran up to us. "Are you afraid to fight me? Are you a chicken like all Meskins?"

I looked to Roberto for help, but he was already moving away from me. I ran, and Roberto ran with me. The redhead was not far behind. He chased us off the school grounds and about a block after that. "Tomorrow!" was the last thing we heard from him.

When we stopped, gasping for breath, Roberto asked what I had done to that kid to make him so angry.

"I didn't do anything to him! I never saw him before! He doesn't like me because I'm *Mexicano.*"

Roberto grinned at me. "Well, I guess you're stuck. You're gonna have to fight him, and he'll probably beat you up bad."

"You're my big brother! You're supposed to help me! You just ran away like a coward."

"Who's the coward? You ran away first. Besides, I'm not afraid of him. It's you he wants to fight, not me."

"Well, you're Mexican like me, so he's probably gonna beat you up too."

I could see that Roberto did not like thinking about that. We walked home in silence, and when we saw our dad, I was suddenly embarrassed at what had happened. *I had run away from a fight!* What would my father think if he knew that?

Embarrassed or not, the next few weeks were pure torment for Roberto and me. Our enemy hunted us during recess and lunch and was always waiting for us after school. We ran away when we saw him, and every school day ended with his chasing us for a block or so, leaving us with that terrible promise: "Tomorrow!"

Fighting him seemed out of the question. He was Americano, and by now we had learned in school that being American meant superiority in all things, just as being Mexican meant inferiority. Our running away served to prove the truth of that idea.

Eventually it happened. I was cornered alone on the playground one lunch period and could not run away or hide. The redhead was there with several of his friends, and I was caught between a school building and the schoolyard fence. They approached me as I backed up, and the redhead pushed me hard, shoving me against the fence. Something snapped and I bounced off the fence swinging and hit the kid right on the nose. He fell and I jumped on him. We rolled on the ground for a few moments, and then he scrambled up and ran away crying, blood dripping from his nose. The other kids ran after him, and I was left alone, exhilarated over what had happened. *He was a gringo, and I had beat him up!* But that feeling did not last long. He was Anglo, and I, a Mexican, had beaten him up. Surely, I would have to pay for that. They would probably kick me out of school.

All that afternoon I kept waiting for the police to come and take me out of the classroom. But as the school day drew to a close and nothing happened, I began to hope that maybe he was ashamed and had not told the principal what I had done. Then another terrifying thought struck me: Now he was going to be really angry at me, and he would kill me when the final bell rang.

As we left the classroom at the end of the day, I explained to Roberto what had happened at lunchtime and about my fears about what the kid would do now. At first he did not believe me.

"*You* beat him up?! You gave him a bloody nose? You're making it all up!"

When I convinced him I was telling the truth, he told me to stay away from him when we walked out of the school building. He did not want to be part of what was going to happen to me once that kid caught me. On the playground, Roberto dropped back from me, leaving me to face the kid alone.

The redhead was nowhere in sight. I walked quickly across the playground (with Roberto about twenty feet behind me), but nothing happened. Once off the school grounds, Roberto caught up to me and walked beside me, still expressing surprise that I could have beaten our tormentor.

The next morning as we walked onto the schoolyard we saw him standing by the swings. My heart starting pounding and I was feeling nauseous, but when the kid saw us, he hurried away, looking over his shoulder.

Roberto stopped. "He's afraid of us!"

"*Us?!* You didn't do anything but run away! He's afraid of *me*," I said, suddenly feeling very proud.

"Well, I'll make him afraid of me too," said Roberto.

At the end of the day, while we were crossing the playground, Roberto was eagerly looking for our former foe. The redhead saw him first and again turned and hurried away. Roberto started after him.

"Hey you, *pendejo!* I want to talk to you!"

The boy started running. Roberto chased him for a moment, then came back grinning broadly. "Oh, am I going to make him pay for what he's done to me! Every day I'm going wait for him. I'll make the little *pinche* cry!"

"What do you want to do that for? Just leave the stupid jerk alone."

"What? Leave him alone?! After what he's done to us? You had a chance to beat him up, now it's my turn."

"He's a jerk!" I shouted. "I don't like him. I don't want anything to do with him."

"Yeah, well it's because I don't like him that I'm going to beat him up. I'll show him what this *Mexicano* is like!"

"Not me. I don't like him. I don't want to be like him."

"You're nuts," said Roberto shaking his head. "Me, I'm going to make him pay."

 Schooling
Part III

By the end of the first school year, I had learned English and eventually I skipped third grade and went directly into fourth. I did all right in school—I learned quickly—but I suspect that I was skipped primarily because of my age and size. A lot of what I learned in school was not what the school was intending to teach me. I learned how to stay out of trouble with the teachers (never raise your hand, speak only when asked to, never ask questions); I learned to fight back when other students attacked me; I learned to laugh at prejudice; I learned to outwit the system—I learned survival.

One day in my third year of school, the principal announced a contest the school was running. Several local farmers were having problems with gophers and had offered to pay five dollars to the kid who caught the most gophers in a one-month period. To collect the prize, we had to cut the tails off the gophers, and at the end of a month's time, turn in all the tails we had collected. The farmers got help relieving their gopher problem almost for free, and the kid with the most tails got five dollars.

Five dollars! I imagined all the things I could do with five dollars and decided I had to win this contest. Of course, every other kid in school had come to the same conclusion, but I was convinced I could figure out a way to outsmart them and take the prize. I just had to come up with a plan.

Roberto and I decided to work together at first. We quickly found out that the task was a lot more difficult than we had thought. Just how do you catch a gopher? We realized that we rarely ever saw a gopher, and we had no idea how to entice him out of his hole. We tried pouring water down a hole, carrying bucket after bucket of water from our pitcher pump to the nearest gopher hole. Nothing happened. We tried building a fire over a hole to see if we could smoke them out. No luck. We found a trap in the barn, and we left it by a gopher hole and checked it frequently. After four days, we found a gopher dead in the trap. About half of the one-month period had gone by, and Roberto and I had one tail.

One tail was not going to win any prize money. Roberto got discouraged and quit the enterprise. But I was sure I could do it. I knew I could beat everyone else if I could just figure out a system. If I couldn't outsmart the gophers, maybe I could outsmart the school. But how?

I took the trap back to the barn. As I was putting it back in the corner of the barn from where I had taken it, there was a scramble and out rushed a big rat. It scampered between my legs and into a pile of stuff in another corner of the barn. I screamed in fright and ran out of the barn, panting for breath. I looked around to make sure no one had seen me running out like a frightened chicken. There were no witnesses, so I headed back home.

That night in bed I kept going over and over the gopher-catching problem and could come up with no solution. With less than two weeks left, I needed to do something soon if I was going to win the prize money. It was too much of a headacher, so I drifted away from it and started falling asleep. Then it struck me. I had it! I knew how to win the contest! It was so simple! Smiling smugly I fell asleep.

For the next twelve days I put my plan into practice. Roberto kept teasing me during this period, asking constantly, "How many tails you got?"

I would respond with, "Oh, I got enough to win five dollars."

He would laugh, and say, "I bet you got one tail, and that's all."

To this I would merely smile mysteriously, and say. "You'll stop laughing when you see me spending the five dollars."

When the last day of the contest came around, all the kids took the tails they had accumulated to turn them in at school. There was a big assembly at which the principal collected the tails from each student and wrote down the number. Most kids had four or five tails—one had seven, which drew "oohs" and "ahhs" from everyone at the assembly, who were convinced he would be the winner. I knew better.

I deliberately held back to be among the very last ones to turn in their tails. I wanted a strong dramatic effect. When my turn came, I handed Major Davis, the principal, my bag with the tails in it. He looked in the bag and his mouth dropped open. He pulled out the tails one by one, counting each one out loud and laying it on the table in front of him. I had sixteen tails. It was no contest.

Major Davis did not particularly like me—he didn't like Mexicans on general principle—but he reluctantly congratulated me and handed me the five-dollar prize. I walked back to my seat grinning so broadly my face hurt.

All the way home Roberto kept pestering me to explain how I had managed to catch so many gophers, and how I could be so disloyal to my brother so as not to include him in my project.

I told him I would think about it, and maybe— maybe—I would tell him how I did it. By the time we got home he was so frustrated it was all he could do to keep from jumping me in anger.

"All right," I said, "I'll show you how I caught the gophers. But first I have to get something. Wait out here and I'll be right back." I went in the house and got my slingshot.

When Roberto saw me with the slingshot, he couldn't believe it. "You can't shoot gophers with a slingshot! You can't even see them to shoot them!"

"I can," I responded. I started looking around for good-sized, smooth stones to use in the sling. When I had several, I went to the woodpile and got a piece of firewood I could use as a club. "Come with me," I told him.

We walked over to the barn. Before we went in I cautioned Roberto to be as quiet and still as he could be. We sat in the barn and waited. After a few moments there was a rustling in some of the stuff lying on the barn floor. Then a rat slithered out, looking warily about. I had already put a stone in the slingshot, and I let fly at the rat with it. The stone hit the rat and it dropped on its side, its legs kicking while it squealed. I ran up to it and smashed it with the firewood. I then took my knife and cut off its tail.

"One gopher tail," I said.

Roberto looked at me quietly, one of the few times I saw admiration and respect for me in his face.

But my victory was bittersweet. That evening Roberto told everyone at the dinner table about my winning the five dollars.

"You won five dollars?" my father asked. "Where is it?"

"It's in my pockets."

"Good. We can use it to buy groceries, and I need a new pair of work gloves. Give it to me."

I handed it over silently. As I leaned forward to give Father the money, I kicked Roberto's shin under the table.

"What's the matter with you?" Mother asked Roberto.

"Ow, ow, ow! I just bit into some food that's too hot to eat," he said, tears in his eyes.

"Just how did you learn to catch so many gophers?" Father asked me. "You'll have to teach me how to do it."

"Yessir," I said, "I will."

 # King Cotton

When we immigrated to Douglas, my dad worked out a deal with his uncle. The uncle had been married to my mom's mother's sister, but she had died eight years earlier. He had recently bought another ranch, two hundred acres with an abandoned ranch house and some outbuildings. He agreed to let us live on the ranch for three years, rent-free, while we fixed the place up and built a herd from the few head of cattle he started us with. After three years, whatever money we made off the ranch would be split with him. In time, we could start paying for the ranch and eventually become its owners. Since this was an agreement between honorable men who were related by marriage, the deal was sealed with only a handshake. No papers were written up or signed.

Having a large family was now an advantage; everybody worked on the ranch. We all got up at sunrise to do our chores before setting out for school. I alternated with Roberto, sometimes feeding the chickens, gathering eggs for breakfast, and pulling up grass and greens for the rabbits, and other times milking the cow. By the time we set out for school, we had been up for two hours. In the afternoon when we came home from school, there would be other chores to keep us continually busy. After two and a half years of hard work the ranch was in pretty good shape and our little herd was growing. We all worked hard, but we loved our ranch and were happy.

One afternoon when Roberto and I had just gotten home from school, Father was telling us that one of our cows had come back to the ranch without her calf and we would have to go look for it, when a black car drove up to the house in a cloud of dust. It was driven by an Anglo man we had never seen, and in the car with him was Father's uncle. When Father saw his uncle, he smiled and greeted him warmly. His uncle did not respond to the greeting. Instead he gestured toward the man with him and told Father that the two of them had worked out a business deal. He told us his companion was a shrewd businessman and an experienced rancher, and he was going to take over our ranch and run it for him. We were being evicted and had three days to leave the place.

Father stood silent for a moment, not believing what his uncle was telling him. I think he first thought it was a joke. When he realized that Uncle was serious, he started to protest, but Uncle cut him off and said the deal was done and papers signed and notarized. There was nothing else to talk about. The two men got back into the car and drove off. It was over that fast.

I'll never forget the look on Father's face. He stared at the dust left behind by the car without saying a word, watching until the last of the dust had settled. Then he looked at Roberto and me with disbelief, as if waiting for us to tell him that it hadn't happened, that he had imagined it, that no family member would ever do anything like that to another family member.

Roberto broke the silence. "Do we really have to leave?" he asked.

Father's face looked as if it were made of dough, kind of gray and formless, and for a terrifying moment I thought he was going to cry. But his face grew hard and his eyes cold, and he answered hoarsely, "Yes. I guess that's the way people do business in this country." He turned and walked into the house to break the news to Mother.

The next few days were like a permanent funeral. We walked around like sleepwalkers, doing chores and packing up to leave our home. I don't remember much about those days, except that nobody laughed and when we talked it was almost in whispers. At the dinner table we all ate in silence, and once, Mother sobbed and leaped up from the table and hurried outside. Father followed quickly, while the rest of us continued to sit, the older kids trying to comfort the younger ones.

Father never talked to or about our uncle again, but he became much more careful about his business dealings in his new country. One of the most important of his beliefs had been shattered. For the Mexican, the family extends beyond the mother, father, children, and grandparents; it includes all those related by blood or marriage, and by religious rites, such as one's Godparents. For one family member to do what his uncle had done to him was almost impossible in Father's view.

Years later, long after we had left Douglas, we heard that the uncle's new partner had stolen all the cattle, stripped the house of everything of value, and disappeared. Shortly after that, my uncle committed suicide. The news did not make Father happy, but I think he felt vindicated in his belief in the sanctity of *la familia*.

We piled our personal possessions into a wagon and moved out of our home and into Douglas, where Father had managed to find a house we could afford to rent in town. He and Antonio, who was now eighteen years old, got jobs on an army base near Douglas, handling and processing thousands of uniforms leftover from the World War, which had ended about a year earlier. The rest of us did what we could. Maria Elena, who was sixteen, got a job as a salesgirl in one of the stores downtown, and Roberto and I worked cleaning out the livery stable once a week and hauling the manure to various households that paid us a few cents for it.

After about six months, the army base closed and Father and Antonio were out of jobs. The family was almost destitute. Then a number of handbills appeared posted on walls all over town advertising for people to go to the Phoenix area to pick cotton. Farmers there needed all the help they could find, said the fliers. The U.S. Army would provide transportation in military trucks for all those who wanted to work. Although none of us had ever picked cotton before, Mother and Father decided to give it a try. Mother, Maria Elena (who still had her job in the department store), and the younger kids (Rosalia, Ernesto, Patricia, and the baby Jose Luis—all those under ten) would stay in the house in Douglas, while the rest of us (Father, Antonio, Teresa, Roberto, and me—Olga, the eldest, had already married) would go to Phoenix to work in the cotton fields. This was the first time the family had ever split up, and it was only desperation that made us do it.

On the day we left for Phoenix, we laid our belongings in front of the house (we were each allowed one small bag, barely large enough for a change of clothes) and waited for the army truck to come pick us up. We kids tried to be grown-up and brave, but I started crying when Maria Elena hugged me just before I got on the truck.

There were two benches along each side of the truck, but there was not enough room for everyone to sit, so some sat in the middle of the floor where the personal belongings were piled, and others, the smaller kids, rode on the laps of their mothers and fathers. We had to go about 250 miles, along narrow roads, often unpaved, in two vehicles that seemed to break down every two or three hours. It took us two days to get to Phoenix. The journey was hell. We sat on the hard benches, bouncing until every bone and muscle seemed to be shrieking. I remember one poor woman who was sick and kept moaning. She had a lot of trouble sitting up on the bench, but there was no room for her to lie down, so her husband kept one arm around her to help hold her up, and with his other hand he kept massaging her stomach. Once in a long while the trucks would stop to let us go to the bathroom or to sit on the ground and eat whatever food we had brought with us, but the stops were never long enough. We spent the night sleeping by the roadside. Finally, we got to Phoenix in the early afternoon of the second day after leaving Douglas.

We were unloaded off the truck, and the first thing I saw was several hundred people in cattle pens and corrals. There were old men and women, young men and girls, and children, many younger than I was. A lot of the little ones were crying and I could hear the mothers speaking softly to them, trying to soothe their fears. They herded us into one of the cattle pens where we huddled together, holding hands. I guess we kids were all scared, except maybe Antonio, who at eighteen was a man and not a kid. As the youngest one, I felt it was important for me to act as adult as possible and not let anyone know how upset I was at being crowded in a corral with all these strangers. No one was laughing and the kids were not playing. It was quiet except for the crying children and a low hum of worried voices.

There were men, ranchers and farmers, sitting on the top rails of the corrals or leaning against them, looking closely at all the people clustered in the pens, talking among themselves. These were the men looking for workers. Soon one of them called Father over, and they talked for a few moments, Father nodding his head vigorously and gesturing over at us. We walked over to him and he told us we had been hired to pick cotton for a man named Mr. Simmons, who owned a farm outside the town of Laveen, a few miles from Phoenix. The farmer went to get a truck to drive us to our new home.

We piled into the back of his truck and Mr. Simmons drove out into a countryside of large fields with rows of green plants on either side of the dirt road.

"That's cotton," said Father.

The truck turned into a narrow lane that ran through one of the fields until it came to a small adobe house that looked like it had been abandoned for several years. We unloaded in the front yard, all our possessions dumped on the ground. Mr. Simmons gave us a bag of beans, some flour, and a couple dozen potatoes. He said he would deduct the cost from our pay. He also gave us each a long, canvas, cotton-picking sack. Then he led us into the house, two rooms of which were livable; a third room had part of a wall collapsed and was sealed off from the rest of the house. The house was completely empty of furniture—no stove, no chairs, no table, nothing.

"There's some firewood in back of the house," he said.

"We will need some light," said Father in his halting English, "a lantern."

"Oh yeah." Mr. Simmons walked back to his truck and took a kerosene lantern from the cab, and from the back of the truck he took a bucket, a kettle, a cast-iron skillet, some tin bowls, and some utensils. "I'll let you borrow this stuff, but don't you run off with it. I want it back."

We carried everything into the house. When we went back out, Mr. Simmons had dropped two wooden crates on the ground. "You can use these as a table," he told us. "And there's water in a cistern behind the house," he added.

He got in his truck. "You start tomorrow morning, picking in that field over by that row of cottonwoods," he said, pointing toward some trees. "Don't start before sunrise." He drove off in a cloud of dust.

"Who wants to start before sunrise?" grumbled Antonio.

Father found some adobes stacked behind the house and had us move them to the front yard where he began laying them carefully on the ground. In a short while he had built an adobe fire pit. It was now mid-afternoon and I was suddenly aware that I was very hungry.

"Teresa, go get some water, clean the beans, and get them ready to cook. Roberto and Rafael, get some firewood and start a fire. Antonio, come with me and we'll start to clean up inside."

It was dark before the beans were done and we were sitting on the ground eating. Nobody said a word while we wolfed down our beans.

Suddenly someone called to us in Spanish, "*Hola.*" Two people stepped out of the growing darkness into the glow of our fire, a man and a boy. "We're camped in a tent over that way," he said, gesturing toward the row of cottonwoods. "We saw your fire and since we're neighbors, we thought we would come and introduce ourselves. I'm Solario Rodriguez, and this is my son, Jacobo." Jacobo looked about my age.

Father stood up and introduced us all, and then in the traditional Mexican way, offered to share what little food we had. They thanked us politely and said they had just finished eating.

Solario sat on the ground and asked if we were experienced cotton pickers. My father answered truthfully that we had never picked before.

"Well, it's hard work," said Solario, "but you'll get used to it quick enough." He laughed. "You don't have any choice."

"It makes your hands hurt," chimed in Jacobo. "Sometimes they bleed until they get tough." He seemed proud to be able to demonstrate his knowledge.

"The most important thing," added Solario, "is to keep going and going. Don't stop picking. Every time you stop it's harder to start again, and you lose money." He seemed to direct this comment at us kids.

"Mr. Simmons said he would pay us a dollar for every hundred pounds of cotton. How long does it take to pick one hundred pounds?" asked Father.

"It's pretty slow until you learn the tricks, but with six of you working hard, you might get two-fifty, maybe three hundred pounds tomorrow. You'll get better at it as you go, and soon might be getting five or six hundred pounds. Just remember, it's best not to stop."

"Mr. Simmons told us not to start before sunrise. What time should we start?"

Solario laughed. "Start about an hour before sunrise, when the cotton is still wet with dew. It's heavier then. Just don't talk or make any noise because we'll be picking pretty close to Mr. Simmons's home and we don't want him to hear us. He doesn't want us to start until the sun is up and the cotton is dry. Come by our tent tomorrow and we'll show you where to pick."

Solario and Jacobo left soon after to go to bed so they could rise early. We lit the lantern and went into the house. We spread three cotton-picking sacks (they were about ten feet long) on the floor, lay on them, and covered up with the remaining three sacks. It was late September and the nights were already uncomfortably cool.

I must have fallen asleep instantly because I remember stretching out on the sacks, and then my dad was shaking me, whispering that it was time to get up. It was cold and still pitch dark when I went outside and saw Teresa cooking potatoes in the skillet on our adobe fire pit. Again we ate in silence.

We gathered up our sacks and set out for Solario's tent by the row of cottonwoods. "Remember," said Father, "no talking or making noise."

Solario, Jacobo, and other members of his family were waiting for us in the dark. "Follow us," whispered Solario, and he walked along the cottonwoods. In the dark, I could make out several more tents and people moving about silently, speaking in whispers as if in church.

"Here," said Solario softly. "Everyone take a row and stay in it. And the *Patron's* house is just over there, so be very quiet."

The cotton sacks were ten- to twelve-feet long, with a strap over the open end. We put the strap over our shoulders and across our chests so that the open mouth of the sack hung beneath our left arms and the sack dragged along behind. This left both hands free to pick, and placed the hungry mouth of the sack where we could easily feed the cotton bolls into it. The plants were about four feet tall, planted in endless rows about three feet apart. Your hands were supposed to be in constant movement, reaching out, grabbing a boll, and pulling it out of its hard shell. I quickly learned why Jacobo had said it made your hands hurt. A hard brown shell encased the cotton, and it was partially open where the shell had split. You reached your fingers into this opening and pulled the cotton out of the shell. At the point where it had split, the shell had four needle-sharp points that pricked your fingers when you pulled the cotton out. In a few minutes, blood was oozing out of my fingers. Since it was dark, I couldn't see it, but I could taste it when I put my fingers into my mouth to try to soothe them. The cold, wet cotton in the cold air made my hands ache, so that when I pricked them, the pain was intensified.

It was like a bad dream, stumbling in the dark, not being able to see, talk, or laugh, my hands hurting so bad I wanted to cry. I kept waiting for the sky to lighten, but time stopped and the morning stayed dark and cold. Finally, I was able to see the people in the row next to mine in the dim gray light. At this point, Solario came and told us to go back to the cottonwoods quietly, where we sat and waited for a few minutes until the sun peeped over the horizon. Then we all headed back to our rows, laughing and talking loudly, as if we were just starting our workday.

I picked and picked, but the cotton just disappeared into the mouth of the sack without making it any fuller or heavier. I remembered Solario's advice: Don't stop;

keep going. So I went and went. I was amazed at how quickly the cold and dark were replaced by blazing sun and searing heat. Now I had to deal with the sweat constantly running into my eyes.

Jacobo was working in the row next to mine, but he was more experienced and was about ten feet ahead of me. I forced myself to try to work faster to see if I could gain on him. I couldn't. He gradually increased his lead. Then he stopped, removed the sack from his shoulders, and dropped his pants.

"What are you doing?" I asked.

"I have to pee," he said. He stepped on the lip of his sack's mouth, pulled the mouth wide with one hand, and peed into it. "It makes the cotton heavier," he explained. "If you have to take a crap," he added, "do it in the sack. You want all the weight you can get."

I stopped and duplicated his actions, peeing into my sack. I would be sure to give the others this tip at lunchtime (we had leftover potatoes for lunch), but I doubted that Teresa would go for it.

I was right. My sister was disgusted when I told the rest of the family at lunch what Jacobo had done, but Roberto thought it good advice and stated he would be sure to do that from now on. We took a half hour for lunch, eating our cold, leftover potatoes without much enthusiasm. That was probably the quickest half hour of my life. We finished eating and had just stretched out in the shade of the cottonwoods when it was time to go back into the fields. I glanced at Teresa, now fourteen, who was sucking on her fingertips and crying quietly. Solario noticed her too and went and talked to his wife, who went into their tent and came out a moment later. She offered Teresa a pair of worn cotton gloves. "Here," she said, "these will help your hands. The gloves will slow you down a little . . ." (at this, my dad looked up), "but once your hands get tough, you can pick without them."

We walked slowly back into the fields, and I headed up my row, a row so long I couldn't see the end of it, just a long corridor of dying green and hard brown stretching forever before me. I found my cotton sack where I had left it, and when I slipped the strap over my shoulder, I was disappointed to see how little cotton there was in it. It wasn't even half full. I started again, hearing Solario's voice like a chant in my mind: *Don't stop, keep picking.*

And so the day went, with me moving slowly, constantly, dragging the sack behind me. The thick plants shut off all movement of air and the huge sun burned above us. I was in a daze, moving like a sleepwalker: *Don't stop, keep picking.*

We quit about two hours before sunset because Father wanted to go to the store and get more supplies. We lugged our sacks to the cotton wagon at the end of the rows, where the foreman weighed them. The six of us had picked 350 pounds of cotton, three dollars and fifty cents, of which Mr. Simmons took twenty-five cents to cover the cost of the food he had given us the day before.

We walked back to the house where Roberto and I immediately lay down on our cotton sacks outside, while Teresa went inside to clean up and rest. Father and Antonio set out on foot to the Laveen general store, about a mile away. I dozed off in the shade and awoke when Father and Antonio returned with more beans, potatoes, green chile, salt and pepper, eggs, bacon, and other items.

The days were all pretty much the same. We woke up well before sunrise, ate in the dark, started picking in the cold darkness, and quit one to two hours before sunset. We did this six days a week, and on Sundays we slept late and tried to recover from our exhaustion. Every Sunday, Roberto, Jacobo, a few other kids, and I would get together and play, the only time of the week we were allowed to be children. But even at play, always in the back of my mind were the endless, stifling rows of cotton that I knew I would be going back to in a few hours. At night, in bed, I sometimes felt sorry for myself and would cry as quietly as I could, wondering if my life would always be like this, wondering where my mother and the rest of the family were, wondering if I would ever see them again. In the daytime, I tried to be adult and not complain.

We had been picking cotton for about two weeks when Antonio got a job as a clerk at the Laveen store. He got paid a dollar and a half a day and did not have to work nearly as hard as he did picking cotton, but the best part was that the butcher in the store was Mexican-American, and he saved bits and scraps of meat, which he gave to Antonio every day and which provided some variety in our diet. The old adobe was beginning to feel like a home: We had gotten another lantern so both rooms of the house had light and some more crates and boxes to use as chairs. Father had also bought a tin tub so we could bathe and some old army blankets that could be hung like curtains between the two rooms so that the Teresa could sleep in one room while the rest of us slept in the other.

At the end of the third week of picking, Father announced that Mr. Simmons had offered him a permanent job on his farm, and we had somehow saved enough money (I have no idea how!) to send for the rest of the family in Douglas. They were lucky; they would come to Phoenix in a train.

They arrived in the middle of the following week. It was such an occasion that we did not pick that day. Father borrowed a wagon from Mr. Simmons and drove to the station in Laveen to pick them up at the train depot. The rest of us stayed home and spent the morning trying to make the place as attractive as possible.

Roberto saw them first, coming down the narrow dirt road that led to the house. He shouted out, "*¡Hay vienen!*" Here they come! and he took off running down the road to greet them. We followed in a pack, whooping and hollering. Maria Elena jumped off the wagon and picked me up, swinging me round and round while she hugged me tightly. I had made up my mind that I would not cry, since I had learned to be an adult. I managed to keep my determination with her, but when Mother reached down and grabbed me, I lost it. I burrowed my face into her breast and cried and cried. I didn't want to let her go— I wanted everything to be the way it used to be. I just wanted to be a twelve-year-old child again. But when she released me, even through the curtain of my tears, I could see all around me the looming cotton plants stretching out forever in their endless rows.

🐦 A Killing

The cotton-picking season was coming to an end, and my dad had begun working as a full-time farmhand for Mr. Simmons, who had provided us with a bigger house across the road from his house. It was in much better condition than the one we had been living in and had a barn in back. We settled in happily.

The town of Laveen was very different from Douglas. It really wasn't much of a town. There was a garage with a gasoline station, a general store that sold food, farm equipment, and dry goods, and a pool hall/bar. When I first saw Laveen, I thought it looked beautiful, surrounded by green farmland and stands of huge old cottonwoods and the hazy South Mountains in the distance. The town was adjacent to a Pima Indian reservation, and the Indians, along with the many Mexican farm workers, were the main customers in town. There were a lot of tough characters around and a lot of prejudice against Mexicans and Indians.

One evening Antonio came home from work talking about a fight in the pool hall. He said an Indian had gotten drunk and spilled some beer on one of the pool tables. The Anglo man who worked in the pool hall was enraged and started beating the Indian with a pool cue.

A Killing

I guess it was pretty brutal. Antonio, who had not witnessed the fight but had been told about it immediately afterward by a friend who had been there, said the Indian was lying helpless on the floor while the employee hit and kicked him. One of the Mexican farm workers who had been playing pool tried to stop the beating. The Anglo hit him with the cue stick, and the two of them got into a fight. Antonio said the Mexican beat the Anglo pretty bad and left him groaning on the pool hall floor. The blood was cleaned up, the tables and chairs put back in order, and the incident was done and forgotten.

The next morning, a Sunday, my dad and I rode a wagon into town to get some seed and supplies for Mr. Simmons. As we came down the street we saw a crowd gathered around the front door of the pool hall. Some of the people were shouting angrily. We hitched our team to the post of the general store and headed toward the crowd. I ran ahead to see what the excitement was. I wormed my way through the crowd and stopped in horror. Lying on the ground was Eduardo, Jacobo's sixteen-year-old brother. Where his chest had been was now a bloody pit. I knew he was dead but his eyes were still open. I was about to faint when my dad grabbed me from behind, picked me up, and carried me away. I didn't realize how tightly I was holding onto his neck until he tried to set me down by our wagon. He had to pry my arms loose.

On the ride back home I didn't cry but my teeth kept chattering. This was the second violent death I had ever seen, and this was a boy I knew, just a few years older than me, someone I had worked and joked with, someone whom we used to tease because he flirted with my sister Teresa.

Father reached out and draped his arm over my shoulders, pulling me to him. "This is a terrible thing," he told me, "but you must not dwell on it. Try to get it out of your mind, or it can make you sick. Think of Eduardo's poor family. We must try to help them through this. Think of your friend Jacobo. He will need your help."

We didn't go home but went straight to the Rodriguezes' camp instead, to let them know, if they didn't know already. As we approached their tent we could hear the keening wail of Eduardo's mother from inside the tent. She came struggling out as her husband and her daughter tried to hold her back. She fell to the ground screaming and crying, rolling in the dirt. Jacobo was sitting on the ground hugging his knees and crying. My dad took one look at me, led me aside, and ordered me to go home. He would stay and provide what comfort he could.

Later, my dad told us what had happened. The Anglo man who had been beaten up by the Mexican the day before had sworn to kill the first Mexican who came into the pool hall. Sunday morning he took a shotgun and sat facing the door, waiting. Eduardo, whose family was leaving Laveen that day to go work on another farm in Gilbert, Arizona, had gone to the pool hall looking for one of his friends to say goodbye. When he entered the pool hall he was blasted by the man with the shotgun.

The Rodriguez family stayed in Laveen several days hoping to get justice for their son's murder, but the killer had fled and no one knew where. The sheriff said he would send out handbills with the murderer's description and name, but the county didn't have the manpower or resources to go looking for him. We all knew there was no chance he would ever be caught.

The other farm workers donated money to pay for a coffin and a burial mass, and the family prepared to move on to Gilbert. They stopped by to say goodbye on their way out.

"*Que vida tan chingada tenemos*," said Solario to my dad. What a screwed-up life we live. "But we must go on. What else can we do, *compadre?*"

Father hugged Solario, then said lamely, "He's in a better place now, you know."

"*Ojala*," answered Solario, "*Ojala*." I hope so. "And may the *puto chingado* who killed him burn in hell." He started to cry softly.

He climbed back up onto his wagon and sat next to his wife, who was sitting wrapped tightly in a shawl, unspeaking. "You have become a friend," he said. "We shall return next year and see you then." He slapped the reins on the backs of his mules, and the wagon started off. Jacobo waved half-heartedly at me as they left.

We never saw them again.

ᴎ Chopping Cotton

Someone was shaking me violently by my shoulders. There was a roar and a wild flapping sound that filled the air, and someone shouting at me to wake up. It was Roberto. For a terrible, confused moment I had no idea where I was. Then it all came back to me. I was in a tent, sleeping with all my brothers.

"*¡Levántate! ¡Levántate!*" Roberto's face was inches from mine, but I could barely hear him above the wind and rain raging outside. "Get up! Don't put your clothes on! There's no time!" I could hear Jose Luis, who was almost three, crying in terror in the darkness. Roberto grabbed my arm, dragged me out of my cot, and pulled me through the tent flap out into the driving rain. I was in my underwear in a wind that was whipping the rain so hard that the drops stung like birdshot. Above all the commotion, I could hear Antonio shouting at me, pressing the end of a rope into my hands.

"Hold on tight to this!" he screamed through the howling storm. "The tent's going to blow away!"

He let go of the rope, and I felt like my thin, thirteen-year-old arms were going to be yanked out of their sockets. But now I understood what was happening. The wind had pulled up several tent stakes, and the entire tent was threatening to go winging away in the wind. Father came running up and took Ernesto and Jose Luis, the two smallest kids, to another tent next to ours, and then came back and grabbed a tent rope. Antonio and I were holding ropes on one side of the tent while Father and Roberto were on the other side.

I don't have any idea how long the storm lasted, perhaps a half-hour, maybe two or three hours, but it seemed to go on forever. I was half-naked, drenched, and totally exhausted when the wind finally died down and the rain stopped. Shivering, teeth chattering, we drove the stakes in again and re-secured the tent. In the tent next to ours, I could hear Mother and the girls moving about. It was almost time for breakfast.

We had lived in Mr. Simmons's house for about a year and a half, with practically everyone in the family working in the fields for him, but since he was an inexperienced farmer, he went broke and had to sell his farm. We were evicted by the new owner, and for the second time in our lives, we were homeless. Fortunately, just two days after our eviction, Father managed to contract with another farmer, Mr. Reilly, who supplied us with two large canvas tents pitched on his farm. We put a wood floor in one of them and strung a tarp across the center of it. Half of this tent was the kitchen and sleeping quarters for my parents, while the girls in the family (the oldest now twenty-one) slept in the other half. The rest of the boys all slept in the other tent.

Roberto, Antonio, and I went back into our tent, dried off, and then went to eat breakfast with the rest of the family. We ate in silence, too tired to do any talking. After eating, Father and the five oldest kids, including me, went outside, got our hoes, and slogged through the heavy mud at sunrise to begin a day spent chopping cotton, swinging our mud-encrusted hoes, clearing the weeds out of the cotton fields.

Heifer

After working for Mr. Reilly for about a year, we were provided with a decent house, and once again we were doing all right. I had just returned from school in Laveen and was going out to pull up some greens and grasses for the rabbits when I saw Father riding toward the house leading a small calf by a rope tied around its neck. I forgot about my chores and ran toward the gate to greet my father. I got to him at the same time several brothers and sisters did. We were all shouting excitedly.

"Where did you get the calf! Who does she belong to? Is she ours? Can we keep her? Ooh, she's so pretty! What's her name?" Father had to stop while we crowded around the calf, petting and stroking. At first she was a little spooked, but when she saw we were all kids like her and meant her no harm, she began to nuzzle and rub back.

She was solid black with a white face and not much bigger than Mr. Simmons's Great Dane. Father had bought her from a friend who had a small ranch near Laveen. "We're going to raise it," he said, "and this winter we'll slaughter it. This little thing will produce several hundred pounds of good beef." We kids kept on oohing and ahhing, ignoring what Father was saying.

Of course, she immediately became the darling of the family. We called her Micaila, a name made up by Jose Luis, the youngest. She was our favorite playmate, and we played variations of "tag," "keep-away," and other kid games with her. She seemed to understand the basic rules and caught on quickly to whatever game we chose. We were all infatuated with her, even Mother—except of course Father, who still saw Micaila as beef on the hoof, and Teddy, our dog, who detested this interloper, a johnny-come-lately who had replaced him as the children's chum. Not that Teddy ever did much besides lie in the shade with only his tail moving every now and then in a feeble attempt to discourage flies. Teddy made a few half-hearted attempts to be playful, but they only made him seem grotesque rather than a potential playmate.

But Micaila was growing, of course, and soon she was so big and heavy that playing with her was a bit dangerous for the smaller kids. Once she stepped on Roberto's foot while galloping clumsily, and at first we thought she had broken it. He went around limping for about a week, a warning to the rest of us to be careful with Micaila. We continued to treat her like a family pet, and she followed us around like a devoted dog, but the games of tag and keep-away got fewer and fewer.

Mother had a carefully tended vegetable garden in the front yard of the house. Father had put up a chicken-wire fence to keep out our chickens, which often roamed free in the yard, and wild rabbits. One day Micaila discovered that if she leaned heavily against this fence, she could knock it over and have access to the garden. By the time Father saw her in the enclosure, she had eaten half the garden.

Father was furious. To make matters worse, when he tried to chase her out of the garden, she seemed to take it as a game of tag, and playfully evaded him, dodging and twisting, and generally having a fine time. When he finally managed to grab her, she had trampled much of what remained of the garden. Father was huffing as he pulled her out, and his straw hat, which had fallen off his head and been stepped on by Micaila, was now once again perched on his head, the crown smashed in. We kids stood watching as he gasped for breath, biting our tongues to keep from laughing. Lord knows what he would have done to us had we been foolish enough to giggle.

Once he had secured her to the gatepost, he shouted at Roberto to get his rifle. "This calf is big enough now to slaughter," he huffed. We kids could not believe our ears.

"Papa, papa, you can't shoot her! This is Micaila! She's our pet! She's one of the family!" We all clustered around Micaila using our bodies to protect her, some shouting, some crying. Roberto, daring not to obey Father, had not gone to get the rifle but had joined our protesting group around the calf. Father roared at him.

"GO GET MY RIFLE!"

We were all crying loudly now, seeing that Father was in earnest. Roberto still did not go to the house to get the rifle, and Father was about to grab him when Mother spoke up.

"Ygnacio!" she shouted. Father stopped and turned to her.

"Stay out of this woman! I will not be disobeyed by my children!"

"Be reasonable, Ygnacio. You are acting in anger. You wish to kill this poor brute who has no idea what she did wrong. She's only a dumb animal, not a thinking Christian. Wait until you calm down before you act."

Father stood glaring at her for several moments, then turned abruptly and stomped off toward the barn. A short while later he rode out on his horse and headed toward the foothills. He returned before sundown, and the subject of Micaila was not brought up again that day. The next day we worked on strengthening the fence around what was left of the garden.

So Micaila got her last-minute reprieve, and life continued pretty much as before, except that Father's jaw got a little rigid every time Micaila came up to rub against him. Then one night, shortly after sunset, we heard footsteps running up to our front door. It was one of our neighbors from up the road, telling us breathlessly that Micaila had escaped from her pen and was now in his yard running around, threatening his garden. We all ran out of the house, Father to try to catch her, the rest of us to protect her from him.

When we got to the neighbor's, Micaila had already left the yard and galloped on toward town. We ran on, shouting her name in the gathering darkness. As we got to the grocery store and mercantile that formed the nucleus of downtown Laveen, we ran into the sheriff and a deputy. They were armed with rifles. "We've got a report that there's a wild bull loose in the area," said the sheriff. "Have you seen it?"

"It's not a bull!" we all shouted at once. "It's Micaila! She's our pet calf!"

"If you see it, shoot it!" said Father.

"No, no!" the rest of us yelled. "Don't shoot her! She's one of the family!" We all scattered in different directions, still shouting her name.

Finally, Antonio and I heard her lowing, and we traced the sound to a house where she was standing quietly in the front yard. We grabbed her around the neck and walked her out to the street. She was now quiet and agreeable, going along without any trouble. In a few minutes everyone was clustered around her, with Father imploring the sheriff to shoot her, and the rest of us shielding her from harm. The sheriff shrugged and said it was not his business what we did with the calf. He and his deputy then left us standing in the street, with all the kids shouting against Father. Eventually we got her back home and secured in her pen.

For a few days it was touch and go between Father and Micaila. She, in her usual loving way, would try to rub against him, and he would snort at her to stay away. But gradually everything slipped back to normal, and Father and Micaila continued to coexist peacefully. Or near peacefully.

Then one day Father was hauling water from the pitcher pump in the front yard to the watering trough used by his horse and Micaila. He had just poured in the last bucketful, set the bucket on the ground, and was leaning over the trough to splash water on his face to cool down. Micaila came trotting up playfully and butted him in the rear, sending him head first into the trough. There was an explosion like a stick of dynamite going off under water as Father came leaping up out of the trough, shouting incoherently.

"Bastard! Dirty no good . . . teach you . . . where's my . . . Roberto! Teach you . . . rifle . . . shoot . . . Roberto!" He was looking around wildly, water pouring off him.

Father ran into the house with a stream of kids following him. He ran into his bedroom and came rushing out with a rifle and a box of cartridges. He was still rumbling unintelligibly as he tried to jam a cartridge into the rifle's chamber. All the kids had crowded around the door, sealing it off from exit.

"Get out of the way!" shouted Father.

"Mama, Mama!" shouted the kids.

Mother came in through the back door and ran to the living room where the battle lines had been drawn.

"This is it, woman!" shouted Father. "This damn calf is meat! It's going to feed us, and that's all!"

"Mama, Mama, don't let him shoot her! Tell him to stop!"

Suddenly everyone quit shouting, and the room was silent except for the heavy breathing of all the participants. We all turned and looked at Mother. She stood there for a moment, then stepped forward and joined us kids blocking the door.

Father howled in rage. For a second I thought he was going to start shooting at us. Instead he just stood staring at his wife for a moment, and then he went limp and let the rifle drop to the floor. "I am nothing in my own home," he said hollowly.

"No, Ygnacio," said Mother. "You are still the voice of this house. You are still the man. But why kill this poor beast in anger? Let's get rid of her, let's sell her, but there is no need to kill her."

Father sat on the couch, saying nothing.

The next day we took Micaila to a friend who had a small ranch and he bought her from us. He made her part of his herd and let us kids go visit her from time to time. The following spring she gave birth to a beautiful little calf. When we asked Father if we could buy her little calf, he let us know in no uncertain terms that that was not a possibility.

⊚ American Dreams

I was sitting at the kitchen table reading a magazine when my brother Roberto came in. It was after eleven, and he had just gotten in from a date with Josefa, his girlfriend.

"How's the scholar?" he asked as he sat down.

At seventeen, I was a freshman in high school, the first one in my family to get that far in my education. My oldest brother, Antonio, and my older sisters, Olga and Maria Elena, had married and moved out of the house shortly after finishing grammar school. Roberto had finished grammar school and was still living at home, but he had no real interest in going to school further. Roberto was working in the Laveen General Store, along with Antonio, who was now the butcher, splitting firewood and delivering it and groceries to the neighboring homes and ranches. He had met Josefa at the store, and they had been going together for over a year. They were obviously very serious about each other.

I loved school and was thrilled to be enrolled in high school. After learning English in first grade, I did well in class and eventually skipped the third grade and went directly from second to fourth grade. Now I got up every school day before dawn, started a fire in the kitchen stove, and then went out and milked our cow. By the time I came back to the house, my sisters and Mother were up and preparing breakfast. After eating, I would walk the three miles to the General Store where the school bus picked up the Laveen kids and took them on a one-hour ride to Phoenix, site of the nearest high school. I would start my day's studying while riding the bus.

There had been a lot of changes in our lives during the past year. We went through a lot of hardship and deprivation to save up enough money to put a five-hundred-dollar down payment on a house in 1925. We had a three-bedroom home on a forty-acre plot with a barn and some outbuildings. The total cost was five thousand dollars, and we were paying seventy-five dollars a month on the mortgage. We still had little spare cash to live on, but we were better off financially than we had ever been in this country. The price of cotton (our primary crop) was high, we grew most of our own vegetables, milk, beef, pork, and eggs, and now we were sacrificing and scraping to pay for our *own* place, and that made all the difference.

And discrimination in high school was a lot less intense than it had been in grammar school, probably because there were so few Mexicans in school and no Indians at all. We dozen or so Mexicans, all boys, generally hung out together, but most of the Anglo kids were friendly enough to greet me in the morning. Occasionally an Anglo student would make a mean comment about Mexicans, but usually they paid little attention to us. In my second semester I made the school baseball team and became the starting second baseman. This made a lot of the other students even friendlier. It was now March, and we had played several games, mostly against the farm boys in the neighboring communities.

Roberto leaned back in his chair and grinned at me. He reached across the table and grabbed the magazine I had been reading. "What's this? Hey, it's in Spanish!"

"It's from South America. Venezuela."

"How come you're reading this stuff?" he asked.

I took the magazine back. "Miss Hays, my geography teacher, gave it to me. See here," I said, turning to the back of the magazine, "these are advertisements put in by big mining and petroleum companies in South America. They want engineers who speak both Spanish and English."

"Engineers! What the devil does that have to do with you?"

"Miss Hays says that if I keep doing well in school, I could go to college and become an engineer. Then I could get a job in South America and make lots of money. Look, here's an ad for a company that will pay seven thousand dollars a year to an engineer that speaks Spanish and English."

Talking about my dreams for the future made me feel nervous and a bit foolish. My dreams about sending money home to my parents regularly, about never having to worry over having enough of anything, of coming back to the United States and buying a big Packard touring car, of buying my own home and marrying—maybe even marrying a *huera*, an impossible blonde like those I saw at school—maybe these dreams were nothing more than silly fantasies.

Roberto burst out laughing. "You're a *Mexican*," he said. "You're like me and like all the other Mexicans we know—*pelados*—no money, no nothing. We're here for *la pisca*, to pick the crops, not to become engineers."

"Yeah, well that's changing. We now have our own place, we pick our own crops."

"A Mexican engineer!" said Roberto, as if the two words could not possibly go together. "Are you going to build bridges and ships out of adobe?" He laughed again.

"Ah, leave me alone!"

"*Orale, 'mano,*" he said. "I've got some real important news! Tonight I asked Josefa to marry me, and she said yes! We're gonna get married in three weeks. What do you think of that, *Señor Ingeniero?*"

I took his hand and shook it. "Congratulations, Berto!" Then it was my turn to laugh. "I can't imagine you as a married man. Can you support a wife and family on the fifteen dollars a week you earn?"

"I've been living on ten dollars a week, since I give five dollars of my salary to the folks for room and board. If we can't make it on my salary, I'll get another job. Besides, we're thinking of moving to California after we get married. There are lots of jobs in *Califas,* and they pay a lot more than here."

"When will you tell Mom and Dad? You know Dad relies on you to help with the cotton crop."

"Well, I've gotta think of my own life and what I want to do. I'll tell them first thing in the morning."

He got up, slapped me on the back, and went to bed.

Much of the next three weeks was devoted to preparations for the wedding. The parents of the bride and bridegroom got together to discuss the cost of the wedding and who would pay for what. It was a short discussion since the bride's parents literally had no money to spare, so all the costs were to be borne by the groom, with a little help from Father. Or so we assumed.

The wedding was held in Sacred Heart Catholic Church in Phoenix, and afterward there was a party at our house in Laveen. Roberto had ordered a huge cake

and some bootleg liquor, while my mom and sisters prepared a number of different dishes for the party.

After the wedding mass, Father and I were standing
outside the church when Roberto came up to us. We
embraced and congratulated him, and then he stepped
back.

"Dad," he said, "can I borrow five dollars to give the
priest as his wedding tip?"

Father was taken aback. "Five dollars? Don't you have
any money with you?"

"No," he admitted sheepishly. "I guess this is as good
a time as any to tell you: I don't have any money at all."

"What! Did you spend all your money for the party
this afternoon?" The Old Man was obviously miffed.

"Actually, no," answered Roberto. "I don't have any
money for the party either. I told the bootlegger you
would pay him when he delivered the moonshine."

To his credit, Roberto did seem embarrassed. Father,
however, was dumbfounded.

"Are you telling me that you have not saved any
money for your own wedding and marriage? You don't
have any money at all?"

Roberto looked glumly down at his shoes. He
nodded.

"Just what the devil have you been doing with the
money you earned at the store?"

"It costs money to take a girl out. I had to pay for gas,
food, dances, lots of things." Roberto glanced over at the
priest, who was standing by the church door. The priest
smiled and waved. "Dad, I really need five dollars to give
the priest."

In a daze, Father pulled out his billfold and handed
five dollars to Roberto, who took it and hurried over to

the priest. They shook hands and the priest laughed gaily, slapping Berto on the back.

When the wedding group arrived home to make final preparations for the party, Father tore into Roberto.

"How the hell am I supposed to pay for this party? Where am I supposed to get the money?"

Roberto's bride turned sharply to face Berto, who was looking very uncomfortable.

"You know I don't have any money," continued Father.

Josefa's mouth dropped open. "You don't have any money?" she managed to sputter. "How can you not have any money? You have this nice home and farm, you must have money!"

"Well, you're mistaken," said Father coldly to his new daughter-in-law. "We don't own this farm. We are paying on it, and the payments take most of our money. I can't even afford to pay for the drinks for this party."

Josefa turned to Roberto, glaring at him. "Well, someone had better pay for this party because the bootlegger is here."

"How much is this going to cost?" asked Father. "I have five dollars left."

"It's twenty-five dollars total," answered Berto.

We all stood silently for a moment.

"Dammit!" said Josefa through clenched teeth. "I want a party on my wedding day, and you promised me one!"

"OK," I said. "I have twenty dollars. I'll give them to you as a wedding gift." I went into the bedroom and took a small wooden box down from a shelf in the closet. I returned to the living room. "Here, take the twenty and pay for the party."

Roberto eagerly took the money and Father's fiver and went to pay the bootlegger.

The party was a success. The food was delicious, and there was lots of moonshine, enough for everyone to get at least a little tipsy, and for others to get dead drunk.

Afterward, Father and I were cleaning up in the living room when he asked me where I had gotten the twenty dollars.

"I've been saving up to buy something later," I responded, not looking at his eyes.

"You're not telling me the truth."

"Miss Hays, a teacher at school, has been encouraging me to study hard and go to college, and then I can go work in South America where they need engin . . . people who speak English and Spanish, and they pay them a lot of money." The words came out in a rush. "I've started saving money to pay for college when I graduate from high school."

He stood there looking at me as if he had never seen me before.

"Look," I added nervously, "here's a magazine she gave me, and it has all these companies that want to hire . . ." I was thumbing through the magazine hurriedly. I looked up at him. He still had not moved. "I was just trying to get money to go to college," I finished lamely.

This time when I looked at him, he looked away. Moving quickly I went into the bedroom and came out with my schoolbooks. Father was still standing there.

"I have to do some schoolwork for Monday," I said quietly. I sat down at the table and opened one of the books.

"You don't have to do any schoolwork," said Father.

I looked at him, and again he looked away. I realized he was the nervous one.

"I'm pulling you out of school. Now that Berto's leaving, I need more help here with the farm and whatever money you can earn by getting a job."

I felt like he had hit me in the stomach, and I sat dumbly, holding a pencil and looking unseeing at the open book in front of me. *Don't cry,* I thought, *don't let your father see you cry.*

He turned to leave, and then paused. For a second he started to move toward me, and then he pulled back.

"Forget about school," he said, his voice suddenly cold and harsh. "School is not for you. Tomorrow I want you to start looking for a job." He walked out of the room.

From habit, I awoke the next morning before dawn after a restless sleep and got out of bed. I lit the lantern in the kitchen and saw my books lying on the table where I had left them. Dully I thought of my chores. I would start a fire in the stove, milk the cow, eat breakfast, and go look for a job.

I took Miss Hays's magazine off the table, turned to the back where the ads for bilingual engineers were, tore out the pages, balled them up, and put them in the firebox. I carefully laid some kindling on the paper, put a match to a corner of one of the pages, and silently watched the blue-orange flame spread until it consumed the paper and the kindling was burning.

The Crash

When I was a kid, music played a major part in my family life. My mother played guitar and sang, and she taught her children who wanted to learn and had musical talent. In the evenings, she often brought out her guitar and strummed softly while she sang traditional Mexican songs—rancheras and corridos—but almost never the songs of the Mexican Revolution, which for her was the main cause of her leaving her homeland and the source of much of her hardship and suffering. I can still hear her voice, low and mournful as she sang of her lost patria, the land of her birth: "*Sonora querida, tierra consentida,*" she would trill—"Beloved Sonora, my hallowed land"—a land she knew she would never return to again.

We older kids, with our memories of Mexico, would join in, but now there were two children who had been born in the United States and had never known Mexico, and two others who were so young when we left they had no memory of it. For them, the songs did not have the passion and intensity that they did for the rest of us. The singing would go on late into the night, and afterward when I went to bed, I would feel a joy and renewal that helped me endure the hardships we had been going through for years.

But mother's health had become more and more of a concern for us. The occasions when she was able to play the guitar were fewer and fewer. One of the main reasons for our leaving Mexico had been her deteriorating health, when she suffered fainting spells that were becoming more frequent. Father was convinced that the chaos and threat of the Revolution had undermined her strength, in addition to wiping out all our savings. So he had taken his family and left his country for a new one.

Mother's health had improved immediately after leaving Mexico. The fainting spells she had been having ended after the ranch outside Douglas became a warm, comfortable home, and she became again the quiet, strong force at the center of our family. After we were evicted from that ranch, and after a year of scrambling for survival in Douglas itself, she once again started becoming frailer and frailer, and the fainting started up again. The first four years in Laveen were a major struggle for us as a family and the fainting continued. Although we found ourselves homeless several times, Father always managed to find shelter and food for us pretty quickly, but the strain on her—on all of us—was unremitting. Then in 1925, our living situation began changing for the better after we put a down payment on a house.

But by now, Mother's health had deteriorated considerably. She was rarely able to go out and work in the garden, or do much housework, or cook meals. Sometimes while eating supper she would lay down her fork, her eyes would roll back in her head until only the whites showed, and then she would slide down off her chair to the floor. Springing instantly to her side, Father would lift her gently while the kids ran around getting a glass of water or a damp cloth to place on her forehead. Father would carry her to their bed, and within moments she would open her eyes and look around confusedly.

This scene was repeated, with increasingly shorter intervals between incidents. As we worried more and more about her health, the family seemed to get closer and closer. Even those who had married and left the home stopped by and checked on her frequently. After we bought our own place, however, she rebounded a bit, and though she never recovered the strength that had been hers earlier, her eyes sparkled and her jaw was once again firm with determination. There was still no doubt who ran the household.

Those first three years of property ownership were the best ones we had gone through in this country. I had a number of different jobs after dropping out of school, I was helping with the farm crops, and the price of cotton (our main cash crop) was high. We not only met all our mortgage payments, we also managed to buy a car and some equipment for the farm. My brother Roberto and I were able to buy a horse and saddle for Father, in a belated attempt to replace Charro, his favorite horse in Mexico. And we even had two tents set up behind the barn for a newly arrived Mexican family we had hired to help with the cotton crop.

Late in 1928, things began to sour again. The price of cotton fell steeply, and I was having a harder and harder time finding any jobs to bring in money. I worked in a cotton mill, which gave me respiratory problems. A doctor told me if I continued working there I would be seriously ill by age thirty. I worked as a cowboy on a local ranch, a job I enjoyed but that lasted only three months. I took jobs irrigating other farmers' fields all night with my younger brother Ernesto and my dad, and after a few hours' sleep, I went to work at some job or another, or helped with our own farm. Money was tighter and tighter, but still we held on, meeting our debts. And then in 1929, the stock market crashed.

The bottom dropped out of the cotton market, and we could no longer sell our crop for the money we had put into growing it. In a couple of months following the crash, we were no longer able to meet the payments on our farm. We had bought the place on a contract with the owner, Mr. Ryan, so Father and I went to see him to tell him we couldn't make the payments. Mr. Ryan was very understanding, and since the whole nation was reeling under the Depression, he offered to let us stay on the farm and make payments whenever we were able. "This will only last a few months," he said, "then we'll be back on track again."

But Father refused. "Never in my life have I accepted charity," he told Mr. Ryan. "Since I was fifteen years old I have taken care of myself, and I have always taken care of my family since I married. I will not begin to accept charity now."

Mr. Ryan argued with him, telling him that it was not charity, that Father would still have to pay the full cost of the farm, and that the payments would merely be delayed for a few months. When I intervened and supported Mr. Ryan, Father gave me a withering look that kept me quiet. I realized that for Father it was not just a matter of accepting "charity"; it was a question of his own *machismo*, his manhood. A man who could not support his family was no man at all. So he steadfastly refused.

"We will be out of your house in three days," he told Mr. Ryan.

We rode back home in silence. The next day, he and I drove into Phoenix to try to find a place to live. We found a couple of shacks on five acres on the outskirts of Phoenix, and the owner agreed to lease the place for twenty dollars a month. We looked at the run-down house and shed glumly. It reminded me of the first place we lived in when we first moved to Laveen and were picking cotton to survive. We were back where we first started ten years earlier, only this time instead of picking cotton we would be growing vegetables and selling them in the farmers' market in Phoenix.

We drove back to Laveen to help the rest of the family with the packing, only to find confusion when we got home. Mother had fainted again and they were having trouble reviving her. With Father holding her hands and Teresa rubbing her temples, she opened her eyes and looked around wildly for a few seconds, and then recognized her husband. She broke into tears.

"¡Ay Viejo!" she sobbed. "¡Perdóname! ¡Perdóname!" She pleaded with him for forgiveness for her weakness, for being another burden for him to bear. Father just reached down and held her until she stopped crying.

The next day Father took his horse and saddle and sold them for next to nothing. There was no room in Phoenix for the horse, and we would not be able to feed it and care for it. Ernesto and I began hauling our possessions to the property in Phoenix, making three trips in one day. On each trip, we took one of the girls and left her there to work on cleaning up the place. Whatever we could not take with us, we sold or we gave to the Mexican family who had worked for us before the price of cotton fell.

After the third trip, we were ready to take the rest of the family, Mother, Father, and two kids. They were all waiting for us in front of the house, except for Father. They told me he had gone out for one last look at the property. I went to get him.

I found him sitting behind the barn, leaning against it, bent forward, his head in his hands. He did not hear me when I walked up, and as I drew near, I realized he was crying.

I had never seen my father cry and stopped short in shock. "Papa," I stammered, "We have to go now."

Startled, he looked up, and seeing me, he turned his face away so I wouldn't see his tears. He made an effort to stand, and I reached down and grabbed him by his arms and lifted him. For the first time I really understood that my father was getting old, that he was frail—so frail!—and I held him tight, wishing somehow to protect him, to make him strong again, to make him once again the man he used to be. And I realized that without my being aware, I had become the one the family depended on, and the weight of that understanding almost crushed me.

¡O, mi padre! For so long you had been the rock in the middle of the stream, unrelenting, holding firm against the tide, our refuge and our strength. And now I would take the lessons you taught me and use them for you, for the family, for myself. I knew I would endure, like you, no matter what; like you, I would survive.

☕ The Widow

I was twenty-one years old and the Great Depression had thrown my family back into deep poverty. My two older brothers had married and left home to raise their own families, so I was now the oldest son, and the responsibility for supporting my parents, brothers, and sisters fell more and more on me. There was almost no work available, and I was always scrambling around looking for ways to get money and supplies to the family. I would go to a government office and stand in line for hours to pick up a sack of free flour. While there, I might hear that another government office was giving away shoes, so I would take the flour home and then go stand for hours in another line to get shoes for the smaller kids to wear to school. I felt like I was running and running but getting nowhere. However, since we grew plenty of vegetables and my oldest brother was working in the Laveen grocery store and would often bring us some groceries—some stale bread or scraps of meat—we always had *something* to eat.

We managed to rent ten acres of farmland for a few dollars a month in Phoenix on what is now 44th Street but was then called Chicago Avenue, just north of Van Buren. We tried doing some truck farming, raising all

165

kinds of vegetables and selling them at the farmers' market in Phoenix. We had an old Maxwell touring car that we used in place of a truck to haul our produce to market. It was our only vehicle, and after using it as a produce truck, I would clean it up and use it to take the young ladies to dances on the weekends.

One day I was driving home from McDowell Road after having spent most of the afternoon visiting a girl I had recently met and was getting seriously interested in. It was late in the afternoon and the sun was in my eyes as I drove, so I ran a stop sign and got hit by another car broadside. The Maxwell was big and heavy, so it didn't roll over, but it was a total wreck. No one was seriously injured, but because of me, the family had lost our only means of transportation and an important source of our income. To make matters even worse, my social life on weekends almost came to a complete end. Naturally, I felt terrible about all the problems my carelessness caused.

There was nothing for me to do but go about finding a vehicle to replace the Maxwell, and do it soon, to keep some money coming in—not an easy task since I had almost no cash at all. I talked to everyone I knew, but no one had any vehicle I could borrow or buy for the few dollars I had. I was under a lot of pressure since the family was now eating mostly what we were able to grow and very little else. Finally I heard about an old Yaqui Indian living in Guadalupe, the Indian village a few miles outside of Phoenix, who had a Model T Ford his son had bought and disassembled in the backyard. His son had lost interest in the car, and the old man wanted to get rid of it.

I drove around Guadalupe until I found the old Yaqui's shack. He showed me the car sitting on blocks behind his house. The larger engine parts were lying on the ground while the small parts—screws, nuts, bolts, etc.—were collected into various cans and little boxes. All the parts were covered by a canvas tarp. The seats were ripped, the cotton stuffing bulging out of the rips, and the headliner was completely torn out, exposing the bare metal of the interior roof. The only window left was the windshield. Fortunately, since the car was on blocks, the tires were still salvageable.

I gave the Yaqui two sacks of green chile, some zucchini and yellow squash, several bushels of tomatoes, some watermelons and cantaloupes, and five dollars. The car was now mine.

I put the tires back on and got a friend to help me tow the car to my house, with the engine and various parts in the back seat. I spent the next several days reconstructing the Model T, practically living underneath it, my knuckles scraped and beaten raw. To my great surprise, not only were all the parts still there, but the car actually ran after I had it back together. It was smaller than the Maxwell, so I took a hacksaw and cut off everything behind the front seat, turning the car into a little pickup with the rear end completely open. It was a junky little truck, and I was embarrassed when I had to pick up my dates for the dances in it, but it was all we had for transportation.

But even though we now had the means to carry our produce to market, the going price for vegetables was so low that we just couldn't make enough money to survive. Bunch vegetables sold for five cents a bunch, green chile for five cents a pound, and sweet potatoes for three cents a pound. There was no way we could get by on these prices, so I had to get some other income.

One day I was working on our little ten-acre plot when a car stopped and a man I had seen before got out. He worked at the state mental hospital just up the road from us and was in charge of the farm the inmates worked on as part of their therapy. He walked up to me and said he had recently leased forty acres about a mile from our land, and he needed someone to farm it for him. He would supply the seed and equipment for planting cotton and pay me fifty cents an hour to do the work. I eagerly accepted and agreed to begin working the next day.

Before I could prepare the land for planting, I had to knock down an old adobe house in the middle of the forty acres. It had been a nice home at one time, but was now a collapsing ruin. I was to finish tearing it down and then plow over it. I took a sledgehammer and a pry bar and got started.

I had been working on what was left of the roof for about twenty minutes when I saw a woman running across the field shouting and waving her arms. She ran up to the house yelling at me.

"What are you doing?" she shouted. "Get down from there! Get down this instant!" She was so angry she was shaking.

I scrambled down the ladder and tried to explain why I was destroying the house, but she wouldn't let me complete a sentence.

"Who told you to tear down this house?"

Again I tried to explain that the person leasing the land wanted the ruin removed, but she interrupted in a quaking voice. "I won't let you destroy it!"

"OK, OK," I told her. "I'll stop if you want me to, but Ma'am, I'll probably come back tomorrow and start again. I'm sorry, but that's what my boss wants, and right now he's got the rights to this land."

She stood with her arms crossed, repeating, "I won't let you, I won't let you."

I felt sorry for her, but I couldn't see why tearing down the house was any of this crazy woman's business. I just wanted her to get out of my way so I could do my job. I looked at her standing there with her arms folded across her chest and wondered what this woman would do if I climbed back up the ladder. Suddenly, without thinking about what I was saying, I blurted out, "I'm sorry this is happening, Ma'am. Today's my birthday, and I don't want any trouble on my birthday." My birthday had come and gone two months earlier, but I was reaching for some way to get her to stop scolding me and let me work.

When I told her that, she slumped and started crying softly. "I'm sorry," she whispered, "I'm sorry. It's not your fault."

I stood there embarrassed, wishing she would just go away.

"How old are you?" she asked.

"I'm twenty-one today," I said.

She sniffled for a few moments, looking away across the fields. Then she looked back at me. "Would you like a drink on your birthday?"

"Huh?! Oh, sure. A drink would be real nice."

"Come on," she said. She turned and started walking across the field toward a large, rambling adobe building that I had noticed before but thought was deserted. I walked beside her. I had heard stories about the house— that the house was haunted by the ghost of an old woman who had died years before, or that an old woman lived all alone in the house, and she was very rich and very eccentric—but since I had never seen her or anyone else around the house, I just assumed the stories were made up.

She got to a back door, opened it, and waited for me to enter. She seemed to be in her late fifties or early sixties, tall and still slender, with graying hair gathered into a bun, and hands with long, thin fingers and skin that showed the purplish veins underneath. She was wearing a black dress with a lace collar and buttons down the front. I wondered if she was in mourning.

We stepped into the kitchen, and she walked to a cupboard and brought out a dark bottle of wine. "This is sherry," she said, "Amontillado. It's not sweet and not dry. Kind of in-between with a nutty flavor." She poured two glasses of the golden liquid and handed me one. "To your birthday," she said, and we both drank. It was the best wine I had ever tasted.

The kitchen was neat and clean, and through a window I could see the house I was being paid to demolish. We finished our wine. She looked closely at me for a moment, and then asked if I wanted to see the rest of the house.

"Sure," I answered, feeling relaxed and warm from the wine.

"First, let me pour a bit more sherry." She filled the glasses again.

The next room we went into had several windows, but curtains had been drawn across them and the room was dark and musty. She walked to one of the windows and pulled back the curtain, releasing a thin cloud of dust clearly visible in the rays of sunshine that poured in. She brushed her hands together and looked around the room as if she had never seen it before. There was a desk near the window, with several books, papers, and an inkwell on it. Everything was coated with a thick layer of dust. The bookcases were full of books so dusty that I couldn't read the titles of the ones I looked at closely. Piles of magazines, newspapers, and more books were scattered throughout the room. I was afraid to touch anything because it all looked so old and fragile, and when I did remove a book from a shelf, the dust made me sneeze. We stood quietly for a moment before she moved hurriedly to another door.

The next room was a parlor with a sofa, a loveseat, and several easy chairs. The drapes in this room were also shut. She pulled them open and the sunlight came in, shining hazily through the dust she had stirred up. There was an old Victrola on a rickety-looking table in a corner and a radio on a stand next to it. There were knickknacks on shelves and tables, little pieces and memories of her life. And pictures. There were pictures everywhere. I picked up a photo of a young man wearing a dark suit with his hair parted in the middle and plastered down.

"That's Leo," she said. "My husband. He passed away six years ago." She took up the picture and looked at it intently. "Six years," she repeated.

She told me they had come originally from Muncie, Indiana, thirty-five years earlier. Leo's father had left him an inheritance shortly after their marriage, and the young couple decided to go west to start a new life. They used the inheritance to buy three hundred acres just outside the growing community of Phoenix. It was mostly desert and not worth too much at the time, but in a few years Phoenix expanded onto their land, which they sold little by little at a good profit, and before long they had no more worries about money.

"The house you were tearing down was built on that land the first year we were here. It was the first home we owned in Arizona. Actually, it was the first home we owned ever. We moved into it in 1897. That was the happiest time in my life."

Oh no, I thought, *she's going to get on me about the house again.* To distract her, I picked up another photograph. It was a yellowed portrait of a young woman with her dark hair arranged like a crown around her head. She was very pretty and was gazing directly at the camera. I recognized the expression. She came and stood next to me, looking over my shoulder, her arm touching mine lightly, a few wisps of loose hair brushing against my cheek.

"Believe it or not," she said, "that's me when I was twenty."

I looked at her and saw the beautiful young girl still there in the aging woman. Her eyes were bright, probably from the wine, and for the first time I realized that she was still quite attractive. "Yeah," I said, "I could tell that was you."

A flush of red ran up her neck and along her cheek. "Do you want to see more?" she asked. "Wait, where's your glass? I'll get some more wine. Wait here." She left.

While she was gone I opened another door and looked in the next room. I must have stood there with my mouth open. There, in the middle of the room, was a Model T Ford. I could tell, even through the dust that covered it, that it was a brand-new, never-been-driven vehicle. Even the tires were new, though by now they were flat. I stepped into the room and ran my fingers along the hood of the car. They left a trail in the dust, revealing the gleaming paint underneath. There was nothing else in the room.

"Do you like it?"

I whirled around and saw her standing in the doorway with two glasses of wine in her hands. She had undone the bun and let her hair loose. "It's beautiful," I mumbled.

"Leo never drove it. We bought it just about the time he got sick, and he never had a chance to drive it. He had cancer."

She walked to me and handed me a glass of wine. "After he died, I didn't have the heart to sell it. It was the first brand-new car we ever owned. I paid some mechanics to take it apart and put it back together in the room. It's been in here for almost six years."

I thought about my rattletrap Ford and all the work and sweat it had cost me to put it together. Now, here I was looking at a beautiful, brand-new car sitting useless inside somebody's house! It just didn't seem right that I should have worked so hard to have a junky old car while she had this beauty gathering dust inside her house. I wanted that car. I needed that car. She kept it in memory of her husband, but she had a lot of other stuff to remember him by. She really didn't have any need for it.

We stood in silence for a while, sipping wine and admiring the car. "I guess you think it's silly, having this perfectly good car sitting in my house." The wine was making her unsteady, and for a moment I thought she was going to cry again, but she didn't. "I guess I live mostly in my memories." She sipped more wine. "I really miss him," she said softly. She turned and walked back into the room we had just left. I followed.

"You're the first man—person—to go in that room since the mechanics put the car together again." She started to sit in the loveseat, then changed her mind and sat down in one of the chairs. She motioned for me to sit in the chair next to hers. I sat down, still thinking about the car. "In fact, you're the first person to come visit me since Leo passed away."

"I always thought this house was empty. I mean I never saw anyone coming in or going out."

"I almost never go out. The grocery store delivers food, and if anything needs repairing, I have a handyman who comes and fixes things."

"It must be awfully lonely being all by yourself for so long."

"After Leo died six years ago, I just didn't care about anything. I didn't really want to live, but I didn't have enough courage to stop living. With him gone, I didn't want to be around other people." She took another sip of wine and looked at me, working to focus her eyes. "I can't tell you how strange it feels to be sitting in this room talking to a man after so many years."

"Well, maybe we can be friends now that I've come visiting."

She smiled. "Yes, that would be nice." She reached for her glass of wine and knocked it over, spilling what little wine was left on the floor. "I'm sorry," she said. "Here you are having to listen to an old lady who's had too much to drink."

"Oh no," I said. "You're not that old."

She smiled, looking like the young girl in the picture. "Thank you. Then you'll come visit again?"

"Sure. Friends."

She rose unsteadily. "That will be nice."

"I gotta go now. That wine's kinda gone to my head." I stood up. "You know, I still have to tear down that house."

"Yes. It's your job. I can accept that now."

She held my arm as we walked back into the kitchen. At the door, she paused. "You will come again?"

"Yes. Can I ask one thing?"

"Certainly."

"Will you sell me your car?"

She stepped back as if I had pushed her. "You want to buy my car?"

"I don't have much money, but I really need the car. I can do a lot of work for you. I can do lots of different things, and I could work off a lot of the cost of the car. I could be your handyman."

"You want to buy my car?" she repeated as if she couldn't believe what she was saying. "Yes, now I understand."

"Yes, will you sell it to me?"

She looked at me closely, her eyes sharp and focused now. "Please go now. No, I won't sell you the car. Goodbye. I'll let you know if I want you to visit again."

"I could do a lot . . ."

The door closed.

I went back to my work thinking about the woman. She must have been very lonely. But she really had no use for the car. If I visited her regularly, I could probably talk her into selling it to me at a good price.

I waited for an invitation to come visit while I worked on destroying the old house, but I never heard from and never saw her again. And as much as I wanted that car, somehow I could never get myself to knock on her door.

⚊ Califas

I stood up slowly, unbending carefully, clenching my teeth to keep from groaning. The sweat ran into my eyes, stinging and blurring my vision. I wiped my eyes with a bandana, and then placing my left hand on my waist, I bent slightly backward, stretching, looking up at the burning sun, again consciously preventing myself from groaning. In my right hand I held a short-handled hoe, about eighteen inches long. In front of me were the rows of lettuce, running out to the end of the world. Ernesto, my seventeen-year-old brother, was in one of the rows next to mine, bent over, swinging his short hoe rhythmically. In the row on the other side was Joaquin, a friend of ours. It was nearly noon, and we had been working in this field since sun-up. How could it be so damned cold when we started, and so stiflingly hot now, the sun so bright it made things look two-dimensional as I squinted looking at the field around me? All about me were strange creatures, grotesque wildlife bending over, rooting in the earth for food. I noticed Smitty, the farm foreman, looking at me angrily, so I bent back down and started hoeing again.

It was 1933 and the Depression was at its worst. Antonio and Roberto, my two oldest brothers, had each married and left our home to start families of their own, and this put extra responsibility on me, and now Ernesto, to bring in more money to make up for the loss of their income. Father was in charge of our little ten-acre truck farm in Phoenix, but bunching vegetables were selling for five cents a bunch, green chile for nine cents a pound, tomatoes for seven cents a pound, and so on. We could eat off our produce, but we could not make enough money for meat and clothes. So Nesto and I were scrambling to find work and bring in a little extra cash. And here we were in Tolleson, some twenty miles outside Phoenix, working for fifteen cents an hour hoeing lettuce.

At noon we sprawled out on the ground, in the shade of some cottonwoods at the edge of the field, eating our cold bean burritos and vegetables from our truck farm.

"*¡Que vida tan chingada!*" sighed an exhausted Joaquin.

I considered the truth of his observation. At this moment our lives were screwed up. When we weren't working like slaves, we were running around looking for slave-work, getting up two hours before sunrise to drive to Tolleson and be here before dawn so that we could be one of the "lucky" ones to get hired for the day. Fifteen cents an hour, minus thirty cents for the gas to get us here and back to Phoenix. I sat up slowly, leaning against the trunk of a cottonwood.

"Maybe it doesn't have to be this way," I started. "Our brother Roberto is in California, in Chula Vista, right outside San Diego, and he says there is more work than there are people to do the work. He says they're paying forty cents an hour, right now, to do farmwork. And that's the lowest pay."

"Oh, man," said Joaquin, "I wish I was in Califas! I could work five days a week, and then on the weekends

177

go down to the beach and lay around watching the girls, the big old *hueras* walking around half-naked like I see in the movies and magazines!"

"You and your *hueras!*" I snorted. "Why do Mexicans think there's something special about blondes? But not me. Give me an *india* any day, with her black hair and brown skin. *La India Mexicana* knows how a man should be treated, not like those blondes who think they're so hot."

Joaquin laughed. "How the hell do you know? How many blondes have you nailed? I want to try one, just once, that's all."

"And just how are you going to get one of these blondes?" Nesto chimed in. "You're so dark you're black. But of course you could tell them you're tanned, and then let them know you work in the lettuce fields. That will get them following you around." Ernesto laughed.

"Ah, go to hell," said Joaquin.

"No," I said. "Why don't we go to California instead? Not to chase blondes, but to get better-paying work. Berto said if we go we can stay at his place with his wife, his kid, and two sisters-in-law. That way we wouldn't have to pay rent—we would just help with the bills for food and electricity."

Ernesto sat up. "Let's do it! Let's go and make some money. We could send money home to the folks and still have enough left to live on. Califas! I've never seen the beach!"

"Yeah!" added Joaquin. "I'd go with you and help pay for food and gas to get there. Let's do it!"

"All right, let's go tomorrow," I urged excitedly.

"Califas, here we come!"

"Get up off your butts!" shouted Smitty. "Lunch is over. I'm not paying you to lie around and jerk off. Get to work."

"Ah, screw you," muttered Joaquin.

It was dark by the time we got home from Tolleson, and Mother and the girls had a hot meal of calabazitas—squash, cheese, and green chile—waiting for us. After eating we went outside with Father and told him of our plan to go to California to stay with Berto and work. He did not go for the plan at first, but soon we convinced him that there was no work in Phoenix that we could do that paid a decent wage. We reminded him of Roberto's letter and the offer to stay with him while we worked for much higher wages than we could get in Arizona. We would not be paying rent and could send the family money every week, more money than we could make here. Soon he was almost as excited about the plan as we were.

Mother was a different case. She still thought of Nesto as a little boy and was dead-set against his going anywhere on his own. Ernesto was mortified and argued bitterly. In the end, I promised that I would be responsible for his welfare, watching over him as carefully as if I were his mother. Father argued for the extra cash, which according to all reports, was readily to be had all over California. Finally she gave in, and Ernesto did a dance while he whooped and hollered in joy.

I got in our Model T and drove over to see Maria, a young woman I had been seeing for almost a year, and about whom I was getting more and more serious. I had always been something of a ladies' man and had no trouble finding women to go dancing with and make love to afterward. But Maria was different. I was dating a wild, very wild, girl when I met Maria, who was the exact opposite of the girl I was dating. She was pretty, so I immediately started putting on my charm with her, but she simply didn't respond. I would try to start conversations, but rarely got more than one or two words from her. The more she put me off, the more interested in her I got. I knew the old charm would work sooner or later. But after a while my efforts seemed hopeless. Yet I wouldn't quit, and in a couple of months I got her to go dancing with me. That was all I needed. I was quite a mover on the dance floor.

Soon we were going out regularly, and it was not long before I lost interest in other girls. Now I was nervous as I parked in front of her house. How would she react to my leaving? Could I convince her that I would be returning soon, and if she waited for me, we could pick up where we had left off? She was saddened by my leaving, but did not question my decision. We sat on her front porch and hugged and kissed and promised to be true to one another.

The next morning Ernesto and I got up early, packed some clothes and some food, and then drove over to pick up Joaquin. Shortly after sunrise we were on our way to Califas, the land of gold and honey. Fourteen hours and two flat tires later, with a one-hour break in the desert to let the overheated car cool down, we were in my brother's driveway in California. I had not seen Berto in over a year, and our reunion was joyful and laughing. His wife, four months pregnant, was cooler. His two sisters-in-law, Dora and Linda, were nineteen and seventeen. Dora, the older of the two, was light-skinned and had bleached her hair blonde. When Joaquin saw her, he glanced at me and winked.

We moved in with them in their two-bedroom house.
Dora and Linda slept in one bedroom, Berto, Josefa, and
their baby slept in the other, while Joaquin, Nesto, and I
slept on the floor of the living room. We had gotten in just
before sunset, and after much catching up on what had
been happening, we ate and talked some more, and eventually everybody went to bed. Nesto, Joaquin, and I lay
awake on the floor for another hour or so, talking in low,
excited voices about what we were going to do in Califas.

I slept little that night, even after everyone else was
quiet and I could hear the slow, deep breathing of Nesto
and Joaquin. Califas! Jobs, money, the beach! And maybe
a huera. No, no hueras. I would be faithful to Maria. As
I lay there I realized that I wanted to marry Maria, and
all I needed was a steady job with a little security. Maybe
here in Califas I would find a job for four or five months,
send money to the folks in Phoenix, and still save enough
to go back and ask Maria to marry me. That way we
wouldn't start our marriage flat broke. I finally fell asleep
fantasizing about life with Maria.

We all rose early the next morning. Berto had just
started working in construction as a *burrero,* a hod car-
rier who worked as hard as a burro. He was getting fifty
cents an hour. Dora, the blonde, was working in the
kitchen of a fancy tourist hotel across the Mexican
border in Tijuana. She worked Friday through
Wednesday nights, with Thursdays as her day off. She
was home because we had come in on a Thursday, and
she didn't have to be at work until six o'clock Friday.
Linda stayed home to help Josefa with the housework
and the year-old baby.

Berto gave us directions to the farm fields and we set
out in our Model T to start our first workday in Califas.

181

From the outskirts of Chula Vista to the farmland was a short drive. The sun had just come up and the light was already golden. It was early September and the peaches, plums, and cherries were just ripening in the huge orchards, and the eggplant, squash, tomatoes, and cucumbers were waiting to be picked. But everywhere on the roads were people, people walking, people jammed into vehicles that made our Model T look good, with all their pitiful possessions piled on top.

"*¡Chingado!* Where are all these people going?"

"They're looking for work, just like us."

"*¡Jodido!*" moaned Joaquin. "Is there enough work for all of us?"

There wasn't. At the first farm we turned into the foreman was looking for people to pick tomatoes, "color picking" he called it, picking only those tomatoes that were ripe instead of stripping all the tomatoes off the vine. This was a much slower kind of picking. They were paying by the bushel instead of by the hour, three cents a bushel. At that rate, I figured we could make about fifteen cents an hour, the same as we had been making in Phoenix. Berto had said farmers were paying at least forty cents an hour, so we decided to go on to the next farm and try for a better deal.

At the turn-off to the next farm there was a sign: "Pickers Wanted: 20 Cents an Hour." We debated whether we should drive in or try for forty cents an hour elsewhere.

"I think we should get some work as soon as possible, and after we make a little bit of gas and food money, we can then shoot for the higher-paying jobs," I suggested.

"OK with me," said Nesto.

"Sure," said Joaquin. "I'm about broke, and I can't go to the beach without any money."

At the farm there was a crowd of men and women standing listening to the foreman who was telling everybody that they were paying twelve cents an hour for picking cucumbers. When one of the men asked about the sign that said twenty cents an hour, the foreman merely suggested that if he didn't want to work for twelve cents, then he should get the hell off the property. We looked at each other and left.

"Twelve crappy cents an hour!" snorted Joaquin. "Shit, we got more than that in Phoenix!"

The next farm we checked at had already hired all the pickers they needed, at twelve cents. By noon, we had gone to at least a dozen farms, but there were no jobs available. Nobody hired for just one afternoon.

As the sun was going down we headed back to Roberto's house, more broke than we had been when we started. We reported our lack of success to everyone at the house.

"How could you not find any work?" asked Josefa. "There are miles and miles of fields with all kinds of fruit and vegetables waiting to be picked. I see all kinds of people working everywhere around here."

"That's part of the problem," I said. "There are too many people looking for work. Haven't you seen all the Okies? They're looking for work too. And the bosses were paying twelve cents an hour, not forty cents like Berto told us. Shit, we got paid more than that in Phoenix."

"So, you don't want to work for twelve cents an hour?" asked Josefa. "Isn't twelve cents better than nothing?"

I almost had to bite my tongue to keep from saying something angry. After all, Berto and Josefa were putting us up. "We'll start earlier tomorrow. And if twelve cents is all we can get, we'll work for twelve cents."

The next morning we left earlier, when it was still dark, and were among the first at a huge fruit farm. They were hiring peach-pickers, paying a dollar and a quarter for a bin three feet wide, four feet long, and three and a half feet high, but again it was "color picking," picking only the ripe fruit and leaving the greener ones on the tree. The three of us working as hard and fast as we could managed to pick seven bins and got paid eight dollars and seventy-five cents, which we split three ways. Back home, we agreed to each pay Berto two dollars and fifty cents a week for room and board, and we each gave a dollar and a quarter of the two dollars and sixty cents we had earned apiece.

And so it went. The work was sporadic; some days we could work all day and make two or three dollars apiece, while on other days we could find nothing. We were each averaging about eight dollars a week. After paying Berto and Josefa, Ernesto and I would send a money order to the folks in Phoenix, usually five dollars. That left Ernesto and me about two dollars and fifty cents a week for our gasoline, clothes, beer, etc. It was pretty tight. And Berto's job was not constant. Sometimes he would work steady for two or three weeks and then not have anything for another week or two. At these times, things got a little tense between us, especially with Josefa.

In late September we took our first trip to the beach. We went on a Thursday morning, Dora's day off. Josefa complained that we should go on Sunday, so that we wouldn't lose any work time. When we explained that Dora wanted to go too, she grumped that Dora could go any time of year since she lived there. We ignored her, packed a lunch, threw some blankets in the car, and crowded into the Model T. Dora sat in the front passenger's seat, while Joaquin, Nesto, and Linda got in back. I could tell from the giggling in back that Linda was a pretty wild kid. Dora was quiet and much more serious.

With our first glimpse of the ocean and the fine sand beach, I finally began to feel like we were really in California. There were brightly colored blankets and umbrellas everywhere, and the smell of salt and fish and seaweed. People were splashing into the waves, and others were running out shivering, and everyone seemed to be shouting happily.

We trudged out and found a spot to stretch out our blanket and food basket. Joaquin, Nesto, and Linda immediately ran to the water line and jumped into the first wave. Dora and I spread our stuff on the blankets and sat enjoying the sights and the sunshine.

Dora stretched out on her back. "Josefa doesn't like you much," she said. "She thinks you're just mooching off her." She sat up. "But I think you're an OK guy. Berto says you got a serious girlfriend in Phoenix."

"Yeah. Maria. I want to get enough money together to ask her to marry me. But it seems like I'm always flat broke and looking for work."

She laughed humorlessly. "Yeah. The things people have to do for money. Well, I think Maria's a lucky girl." She stood up and started toward the water. "Come on in."

I followed behind her, admiring the way her hips swayed and the smooth movement of her buttocks. I had been a long time without a woman, but I had better be very careful in my brother's house.

After the initial shock of cool water and the taste and sting of the saltwater, I lay back and floated for a while, feeling more at ease than I had felt for quite a while. When I went back to our spot, I noticed that the people on one side of us had left and moved on farther down the beach, and the people on the other side were gathering up their stuff and getting ready to move also. I sat down, aware of the occasional hostile looks I was receiving. After the others had come back to our blanket, we started spreading out our lunch when we noticed a cop walking down the beach toward us. He walked up to the blanket and stood over us looking down.

"Does anybody here speak English?" he asked.

We told him we all did. Then he asked if we were American citizens. We told him we were. He asked for some sort of proof. I showed him my Arizona driver's license. He then wanted to know what I was doing in California. I said we were looking for work, and he snorted in disgust.

"You people think you can come here and take jobs away from hardworking Americans by working for wages no decent person can live on."

"We're Americans too," said Joaquin.

"Prove it," said the cop. "Show me some identification."

"I don't have any with me," answered Joaquin. "I left my wallet at home."

"Then maybe I should arrest you and turn you over to Immigration. Maybe you can prove to them that you're an American citizen."

"Jesus!" I said. "We're not doing anything to anybody. We just wanted to come to the beach."

The cop looked at me quickly, his eyes cold and harsh. "Don't play the wiseguy with me! You don't think I can take you in? I'll tell you what: If you aren't off this beach in five minutes, we'll find out if I can take you in. Go back to wherever the hell you live and leave this beach for decent people."

He stood and watched while we quietly picked up our stuff and headed back to the car. Joaquin was so angry I was worried he would lose control and get us in real serious trouble. But he had to satisfy himself with a continuous string of profanity all the way back to Berto's.

As the summer ended and the fall came on, picking jobs became more and more scarce. There was some work planting and weeding the cool-weather crops like lettuce and spinach, but not much. I managed to get hired as a burrero by the same construction company that Berto worked for, while Joaquin and Nesto continued doing whatever jobs they could find.

By early December I was very homesick, thinking about Maria, about my folks in Phoenix, and about the coming Christmas. There was less and less construction, and fewer farm jobs, so there was less and less money, which created more tension between Josefa and us. Berto was obviously embarrassed whenever she made nasty remarks about freeloading relatives, but she was in too much control over him for him to say or do anything. I was feeling miserable.

A few days before Christmas, Joaquin told me about a place in Tijuana that the other farm workers talked about, a whorehouse where for a dollar and a half a man could spend a few minutes with a woman.

"Everybody goes there," said Joaquin. "And they got some *hueras* working there. Man, I'm gonna go Friday. I haven't been laid since we left Phoenix. Maybe I can get me a *huera* yet."

I was feeling so sad and lonely that I agreed to go with him.

The next night the three of us drove the few miles to Tijuana, making sure we had documents to certify our American citizenship. After our experience on the beach, we had become pretty careful. We found the place, a ratty old "hotel" called "The Rialto." We went in and paid our dollar and a half and were told to wait our turn in the lobby. There were six men ahead of us. Every few minutes a man would walk down the stairs, the desk clerk would call out a room number, and someone in the lobby would get up and walk up the stairs. And then it was my turn.

I went upstairs and down the hall until I came to the right door. I opened it and stepped in. The woman was standing naked, with her back to me, washing up in a basin on a mirrored dresser. She was blonde. She turned to face me and we both froze for an instant.

"Oh God!" she said, trying ineffectively to cover up her nakedness with two hands. Dora stood, eyes wide, mouth gaping.

We both spoke at the same time. "Please don't tell Berto ..." "Please don't tell Maria ..." And then we stood silent.

"We needed the money," she said, "and I couldn't get another job, and they told me if I bleached my hair I could make a lot of money ..." She sobbed softly. "Please don't tell."

"No, no, I won't tell anyone if you don't. It's just been so long since I've been with a woman."

She sat on the bed, and there was an awkward silence. "I guess you've already paid, huh?"

"Yeah."

Another short silence. "Well, since you've already paid ..."

I walked toward her, suddenly intensely excited.

On the way home both Joaquin and Nesto were boasting about their "performance." I was feeling more depressed than ever.

"Hey," said Joaquin to me. "Did you get a blondie?"

"Why don't you just shut the hell up about blondes!" I exploded, shocking Joaquin into silence with my anger. Nobody talked anymore.

When we got back to Berto's, I announced that I was leaving for Phoenix right then, just as soon as I got my gear packed. If Nesto and Joaquin wanted to come with me and be home for Christmas, they were welcome, but I had had it with Califas. They were both jubilant about our leaving, almost as happy as Josefa when she heard the news. She was smiling, and even trying to be pleasant. I assured Berto and Josefa that my desire to leave had nothing to do with them and their hospitality, but that I missed Maria and my family. They said they understood.

As we were getting our stuff together, Nesto said he was feeling a little sick with an upset stomach and sore throat, but he made it clear that he wanted to leave as soon as possible. We said our goodbyes and were on the road before ten. Nesto was in the back seat, and after a while he started groaning, and then he asked me to stop. He got out of the car and vomited by the roadside. By now it was terribly cold with the wind blowing very hard. He lay back in the seat and I covered him with a couple of blankets. His teeth were chattering and he kept wrapping his arms around his stomach and groaning. He would fall asleep and lie twisting and turning, mumbling incoherently.

Sometime between one and two in the morning, the Model T started sounding like a washing machine with an unbalanced load. I pulled over to the side immediately, but I knew it was already too late. We had a burned-out bearing in the middle of the desert, with El Centro about forty miles behind us and Yuma, Arizona, about twenty-five miles ahead. And it was cold, very cold. The wind was blowing across the desert with almost nothing to serve as a windbreak. And in the back seat, my brother was twisting and turning, moaning softly. Joaquin, who had been sleeping in the passenger seat, woke up. I explained our situation to him, and we both sat and stared out the windshield into the darkness.

"*Pinche Califas!*" grumbled Joaquin. "How many miles to Arizona?"

"Around twenty."

"*¡A la chingada con Califas!*" he gritted through his teeth.

"Well," I said, "Hold my hat. I've gotta check the engine and see what we got."

I grabbed my toolbox and crawled under the car with a flashlight. I lay there shivering for a moment, and then I took off the oil pan. It was bone dry. All of the oil had leaked and one of the bearings had burned out. I did not have another bearing. I crawled out from under the car and got back in beside Joaquin. "It's the bearing."

He groaned. Behind him, Nesto sat up slowly. "Where are we? Are we in Phoenix?"

"No. We got some car problems. Lie down brother. Cover up with this blanket. Don't worry, I'll take care of the car."

I sat there, holding onto the wheel, just wishing I could forget about the car and hoping the problem would go away.

"Here's your hat," said Joaquin.

I took it, ran my finger along the inner hatband as a matter of habit, and put it on. Then I thought of the leather hatband. I took off the hat and removed the band. It wasn't a bearing, but it was better than metal against metal. I crawled back under the car with the hatband in hand.

Again the cold was a shock as the wind whistled across the road and under the car. I started to remove the damaged bearing.

My fingers ached with cold, and whenever my wrench would slip, I would bang a hand against the cold metal of the engine and waves of pain would come over me, and I would lie there with my eyes clenched, shivering, cussing the car, the wind, Califas, my whole damned life. Would I always be scrambling for money, leaving home, working like a mule, never getting anywhere? Then I would think that I didn't have the time or the luxury to feel that way; my brother was sick and needed help, and I had promised Mother I would care for him. So I would take the wrench and start again, determined to finish the job, until the next time the wrench slipped and I banged my hand.

Finally, I replaced the bearing with the rolled-up strip of leather from my hatband. I had a gallon of oil in the car, so we poured it in and were on our way again. After about fifteen miles, all the oil had leaked out and the leather had burned up. We were stranded again. Once more I sat there, holding on to the wheel, just wishing this bad dream would go away. In the back seat, my brother was groaning.

"Joaquin," I said. "I'm going to go on walking toward Yuma and see if there is place that's open. You stay here with Nesto, and see if you can keep him warm."

I set out in the bone-chilling wind. I had no hope of finding anything, but I felt I should do something. But to my astonishment, I had been walking for only about fifteen minutes when I saw a light far ahead. My hopes went up and I started walking faster. Soon I was running. It was an all-night service station run by an angel, a grimy, oil-smeared angel with a gimpy leg, but an angel anyhow.

He had a bearing, oil, and a gasket for the oil pan. I returned to the car and crawled under it again. Once more I removed the pan and replaced the missing bearing. Once again I lay cursing my life every time the wrench slipped. In the middle of one of these cussing sessions, a thought popped into my head. I was going to ask Maria to marry me as soon as I got back to Phoenix. To hell with waiting until I had saved up some money, or waiting until I had a secure job. I was never going to save money, I would never have any security, I would always be scrambling. I didn't have a damn thing to offer her but myself. If she really wanted me, she would say yes.

Suddenly I felt good. I was going to get the car going, I would get Nesto home, and I would go see Maria. I put the pan back on and got back in the car. It wouldn't start. I kept cranking the engine, but it just wouldn't turn over. I had tightened the bearing too much.

Again I sat there holding the wheel tightly. "Damn it!" I shouted at Joaquin. "I'm not going to take that goddamned pan off again!"

Nesto groaned. "Mama, is that you?"

"Let's push it," I said to Joaquin. "Maybe we can get the car going fast enough that we can loosen the bearing enough to start." We pushed. And pushed. I kept jumping in, putting it in gear, and popping the clutch, but it was no go. Too tight.

After a half an hour, when the sun was coming up, we saw a car coming in the distance. We got a push from a couple of young guys driving home for Christmas. They got us going fast enough for our car to start. They waved, called out a Merry Christmas, and left us behind. Since the bearing was so tight, we could only go at about twenty to twenty-five miles an hour. We drove into our home in Phoenix fifteen hours later, as everyone was getting ready for a late Christmas Eve dinner.

Since no one had expected us to be home, we turned out to be everybody's best Christmas present. Even Nesto, sick as he was, managed to smile and wish everyone a Merry Christmas before being put in bed by his worried mother. After our happy greetings, I took Joaquin home to his family.

He stood by the car window and thanked me for the trip to Califas. At that, we both laughed. "*¡A la chingada con Califas!*" he said, and we laughed some more. "What do you do now?" he asked.

"I'm gonna go to Maria's right now and ask her to marry me."

Joaquin gave a holler and stuck his hand in the window to shake mine. "All right! Man you got a great girl. She'll be a really good wife."

"Wait! She hasn't said she'll marry me yet. I don't have anything to offer her, no money, no job, nothing. Why would she want to marry someone like me?"

He laughed. "Don't worry. She'll say yes, don't you worry about that. You'll get married and you'll be all right. Don't worry about that. That's for sure—you'll be all right."

Epilogue

Maria and I did marry and raise a family. I continued doing all sorts of odd jobs for the first few years of our marriage, but eventually I started working in construction and by 1940, I was a union carpenter with steady work during the boom years of the 1950s. In 1948, my brothers and I bought a lot in Phoenix, on which we built a house for our folks. Ten years later, Mother passed away. Father survived her by five years and then he went to join her.

Today I am retired and living on my union pension, social security, and the rent from one of two houses we own. We had five children, two daughters and three sons. My youngest son died in Viet Nam, and my oldest son is a retired schoolteacher. One daughter still teaches in elementary school, the other lives in Maryland with her husband, a retired Air Force colonel. The youngest surviving son is a petroleum engineer—in South America.